Long, Tall
Christmas

Center Point
Large Print

Also by Janet Dailey and available from
Center Point Large Print:

Christmas in Cowboy Country
Merry Christmas, Cowboy
A Cowboy Under My Christmas Tree

Long, Tall Christmas

JANET DAILEY

CENTER POINT LARGE PRINT
THORNDIKE, MAINE

This Center Point Large Print edition is published
in the year 2015 by arrangement with
Kensington Publishing Corp.

The text of this Large Print edition is unabridged.
In other aspects, this book may vary
from the original edition.
Printed in the United States of America
on permanent paper.
Set in 16-point Times New Roman type.

ISBN: 978-1-62899-747-7

Library of Congress Cataloging-in-Publication Data
Dailey, Janet.
    Long, tall Christmas / Janet Dailey. —
    Center Point Large Print edition.
        pages cm
    Summary: "Widowed Kylie Wayne moves back to small-town
Branding Iron, Texas, to help her aging aunt on her ranch. But when an
early storm threatens Kylie's dream of a perfect Christmas for her kids,
it's up to a long, tall Texan with a bad boy's charm to rope some
holiday cheer"—Provided by publisher.
    ISBN 978-1-62899-747-7 (hardcover : alk. paper)
    1. Large type books. 2. Christmas stories. I. Title.
PS3554.A29L574 2015
813′.54—dc23
                                                                    2015032464

Long, Tall Christmas

Chapter One

December 22

"Ouch!" The hot cookie sheet slipped out of Kylie Wayne's hand and clattered to the linoleum. Tears flooded her baby blue eyes—not so much for her seared thumb as for the Christmas cookies, which were not only broken and scattered, but also burned to a crisp.

"Oh, dear!" Her great-aunt, Muriel, bustled into the kitchen. "What happened?"

Kylie ran cold water over her thumb to ease the pain. "I smelled the cookies burning and grabbed them with that old brown oven mitt. There must've been a hole in it."

"Heavens, I'm sorry. I've been meaning to mend that hole." Aunt Muriel shook her silvery head. "Those poor cookies! They were so pretty! And you worked so hard on them!"

Kylie sighed in silent agreement. She'd barely had time to unpack the car, but with Christmas less than three days off, and her two children moping like jailbirds, she'd felt the need to create some holiday spirit.

She'd found some old cookie cutters and spent the past hour mixing, rolling, and cutting the dough into Christmas bells, angels, reindeer, and stars. They'd been perfect when she'd slid them into the oven to bake. But she had yet to master the workings of Aunt Muriel's sixty-year-old electric stove.

"I don't understand it," she muttered. "The recipe said fifteen minutes at three hundred seventy-five degrees. When I checked after ten minutes, they were already black and smoking."

"That old oven's always cooked hot," Aunt Muriel said. "I've gotten used to it over the years. You will, too, dearie."

"Yes, I suppose I'd better." Kylie bent to pick up the mess. The offer of a home for herself and her children, in exchange for looking after her grandfather's sister on her small Texas farm, had come as a godsend. At seventy-nine, Aunt Muriel was a sweetheart—a bit absentminded, but pretty much able to do for herself. It was the rest of it—coming home to Branding Iron, Texas, after fifteen years as an army wife—that weighed Kylie down. It was as if she'd come full circle, back to the place she'd been so glad to leave behind after high school. As for her children, she hadn't seen a single smile since their loaded station wagon pulled away from their foreclosed house in San Diego.

She swept the last of the blackened crumbs into the dustpan and dumped them into the trash. "I guess there's nothing to do but start over from scratch. Maybe this time you can help me with the stove."

"The Shop Mart in town has cookies," Aunt Muriel said. "You could just buy some."

"It's not the same. The smell of fresh-baked sugar cookies, and the fun of helping ice them—that's the kind of Christmas we used to have. I want to bring some of that back for Hunter and Amy. After last year . . ."

Her voice trailed off. Last Christmas, the first after her husband Brad's death in Afghanistan, Kylie had been in no mood for celebration. It had been all she could do to toss a few decorations on an artificial tree and wrap a few last-minute gifts for her son and daughter. But this year nothing would stop them from having a *real* Christmas. She would see to it.

"I know it won't be the same without their father," she said. "But they've been through so much. Whatever it takes, I owe them a good Christmas."

"And what do you owe yourself, dear?" Muriel had a knack for asking odd questions—questions Kylie had no idea how to answer.

This time she was saved by the distant *thrum* of a motorcycle speeding down the nearby road. The sound grew closer and louder, its masculine thunder roaring in her ears as it passed the house and faded away toward town. She'd heard it late yesterday afternoon, too, right after they'd arrived here. The sound was so loud and invasive that it seemed to shake the walls of the little farmhouse.

"Good grief, that noise would wake the dead! How do you put up with it?" she asked.

Muriel smiled. "I've rather grown to like it. It makes me feel safe, knowing the cowboy's close by, looking out for me and for Henry."

Henry was Muriel's longtime hired man, who lived in a trailer out back. He appeared to be about the same age as his employer. No doubt both of them could use looking after. But a cowboy on a motorcycle struck Kylie as an unlikely guardian angel.

"I call him 'Cowboy' because I can never remember his name," Muriel said. "It's Sean or maybe Sam . . . something like that. But he says he doesn't mind answering to Cowboy."

"So he lives around here?"

"He owns the ranch to the west. Every few days, or whenever we need him, he drops by to check on us and help Henry with the heavy work. He won't take any money for it, but he never turns down an invitation to a home-cooked supper."

Kylie was already feeling protective of her great-aunt. What if this so-called cowboy was trying to charm Muriel out of her farm, or maybe her life savings?

"So when will I be meeting your cowboy?" she asked.

"Oh, he's bound to show up sometime soon. He's about your age, dear, and—oh, my stars—what a man! Tall and broad-shouldered, with dark, curly hair and deep brown eyes . . ." Muriel sighed. "I can't imagine why he's not married. Goodness, if I were fifty years younger, I'd go after him myself!"

"Aunt Muriel!" Kylie was mildly shocked.

"Don't look at me like that, girl! I may be old, but I've got eyes in my head. I appreciate a handsome man as much as the next woman, even if all I can do is look. And, believe me, that cowboy is an eyeful!" Muriel tilted her head, giving Kylie a glimpse of the spritely young woman she'd once been—a woman who'd devoted half a lifetime to caring for her invalid father, passing up any chance she might've had to marry.

"Now, with you it's different," she said. "A pretty thing like you could do a lot more than look if you set your mind to it."

"Forget that." Kylie put the broom back in the corner and began gathering ingredients for a new batch of cookies. "I've got my hands full with two growing children who miss their dad. The last thing I need is a new man in my life—especially some cowboy who goes roaring by on a noisy old motorcycle."

"Well, dear, you won't be hearing that noise much longer. He puts the motorcycle away once

11

it starts snowing—and the weatherman on TV is predicting a big storm this weekend. An honest-to-goodness blue norther!"

"What?" Kylie's gaze flew to the window with its view of dull gray skies and vast sweeps of yellow grass. This part of the high Texas plain didn't get much snow. But storms had been known to happen here—the locals called them "blue northers" because they blew in from the north, and the cold air they left in their wake could turn a body blue. Kylie remembered a few times from her girlhood when blizzards had closed roads and schools and stranded livestock in the fields. This was no time to be low on supplies, especially with children in the house and Christmas around the corner. The cookies would have to wait while she made a run to town.

Brushing a dab of flour off her blouse, she slipped on a fleece jacket and grabbed her purse off the counter. "We'll need to stock up before the storm gets here," she said. "I'll pick up the makings of Christmas dinner. Oh—and we'll be wanting a Christmas tree. Does Hank Miller still sell them in that lot next to his feed store?"

"He does. But you might have to take leftovers. He'll be out of the nicer trees by now."

"Is there anything else you need?"

"No, dearie. Just get whatever you and the children will like. You know, it's a shame you didn't get here last week. The town had its little

Christmas parade, complete with Santa in his sleigh and the high-school marching band. Abner Jenkins is still playing Santa—he's perfect for the job, doesn't even need any padding in his suit. Of course, with no snow, the sleigh had to be pulled on a trailer by those big draft horses of Abner's, but it was still a nice way to get into the holiday spirit."

The old woman turned away, then paused. "Oh, and you would have loved the Cowboy Christmas Ball last Saturday night. It's like something right out of the Old West. The men wear cowboy gear, the ladies wear long skirts. We always have a live band, and the food . . . oh, my!" She gave Kylie a wink. "There's many a romance that started at that dance. Too bad the next one's a year away."

"I do believe I can wait." Kylie fumbled in her purse for her keys.

Muriel walked into the living room, turned on her favorite soap opera, and settled in the rocker with the gray wool sock she was knitting. The click of her needles blended with the sounds of the TV as Kylie stepped outside and closed the door.

The December air was calm but chilly. The smell and taste of coming snow awakened memories from Kylie's childhood. Her family had lived in town then, and her father had taught math at the high school. Now her parents, like

Brad, were gone, lost in a tragic car accident ten years ago. She was alone with no close family except her children and her great-aunt, Muriel.

Hunter and Amy had gone outside after lunch. As she rounded the house, Kylie could see them sitting on the corral fence, both of them hunched over their phones, most likely playing games or texting the friends they'd left behind in California.

Kylie waved to catch their attention. "Anybody up for a trip to town?" she called.

Hunter glanced up, shook his head, and returned to his phone. One day the boy would look a lot like his stocky, sandy-haired father. He might even have Brad's easy smile and outgoing charm. But right now, he was going through a rough time, and being thirteen didn't make it any easier. After Brad's death, Hunter had withdrawn into a shell. With the move from California, that shell had all but closed around him.

"How about you, Amy?" Kylie asked her eleven-year-old daughter.

"Get real, Mom! We just spent four days from hell in that car! Anyway, there's no place to hang out in town, not even a mall. It's boring, boring, boring! I hate it here!"

Amy, blond and pretty, was dealing with the changes in her own way. She'd always been a thoughtful, tenderhearted child. Was this onset of brattiness an attempt to hide her feelings, or was

14

she just moving into her teen years a little early?

Never mind, Kylie told herself. She needed a break, and her children would be fine here without her. She could see Henry over by the barn, staying close enough to keep an eye on them without getting in their faces. A good man, Henry Samuels. He'd been working on this little farm for as long as Kylie could remember. She knew she could count on him.

Only as she settled into the driver's seat and started the station wagon did Kylie realize how tired she was. For the past nineteen months, since Brad's death, she'd done her best to put a brave face on things—dealing with her own grief and the children's, struggling to make ends meet on her widow's benefit, looking for a job and failing to find one, packing the station wagon and driving two grumpy youngsters all the way from California to Texas.

Right now, all she wanted was to crawl into a warm, safe bed, burrow under the quilts, and then sleep around the clock. But she couldn't even think about resting—not with Christmas almost here and so much to be done.

At least she wouldn't have to shop for gifts. She'd ordered everything online from a company that guaranteed Christmas delivery. Since she'd used Muriel's address, the packages should be arriving any day now. She had sweaters, computer games, and new phones for the children, as well as a warm cashmere shawl for Muriel and new leather gloves for Henry.

The seven-mile road to town cut a straight line across flat pastureland, dotted here and there with clustered trees and buildings that marked farms or small ranches. Beef cattle, more black Anguses these days than the red-coated Herefords Kylie remembered, grazed in the fields. Aside from that, not much appeared to have changed. Driving down Main Street, on her way to Aunt Muriel's, she'd noticed the new strip mall with a supermarket, a craft shop, and a chain pizza parlor. But the bones of the town—the schools, churches, and modest homes—were much the same as when she'd left for college, where she'd met Brad and married him at nineteen.

But just because she'd come home didn't mean she had to live in the past. Turning on the car radio, she fiddled with the dial until she found the only clear station, which played country-music oldies—one more thing that hadn't changed.

Hank Miller's feed store was on the way into town. She would buy the Christmas tree first. If it wouldn't fit in the back of the station wagon, maybe Hank could tie it on the top. She'd wanted a nice, fresh bushy pine, but she would settle for whatever she could get. When she'd packed for the move, she'd boxed the precious decorations that went back to the children's babyhood, one for each year of their lives. Putting them on the tree again would make Aunt Muriel's two-story clapboard house seem more like home.

Singing along with Elvis's "Blue Christmas," she pulled up to the tree lot.

The song died in her throat.

The makeshift fence was still rigged around the tree lot. Pine needles and a few broken branches littered the ground. Aside from that, the lot was empty. A sign on one of the posts read, SOLD OUT.

Kylie struggled to ignore the dark knot in her stomach. She couldn't just give up. The tree was too important. Maybe the market would have a few. They might be more expensive, but she was desperate enough to pay any price.

Still hopeful, she pulled into the crowded Shop Mart parking lot. The place was busy this afternoon—most likely with folks stocking up for the storm or buying extra food for Christmas. Kylie drove along the rows of parked cars, SUVs, and pickups, looking for an empty spot. Every space was filled. But on her second time through, she saw a woman loading groceries into the back of a van. With impatient drivers honking behind her, Kylie waited. When the van pulled out, she swung into the parking place. So far, so good. She grabbed her purse and climbed out of the station wagon. Maybe luck would be with her this time.

But she saw no Christmas trees in front of the

store. If they'd ever been here, they were gone. As a last resort, Kylie asked a clerk about boxed artificial trees. There were none. For a moment, she weighed the wisdom of driving to the next big town, sixty miles to the north. But there was no guarantee she'd find a tree there, either. And with the sky already darkening, she didn't want to be caught on the road when the storm swept in.

At least the store had plenty of provisions. Kylie found a hickory-smoked ham and some potatoes and carrots to save for Christmas dinner. She also stocked up on the children's favorite cereals and the mac-and-cheese mix they liked. They'd need all the basics—including milk, eggs, butter, sugar, juice, bread, pancake mix, syrup, and bacon, as well as tuna, mayonnaise, lettuce, and pickles for sandwiches. As an afterthought, she slipped some Christmas candy and small trinkets in with the essentials. Aunt Muriel had offered free rent, but that didn't include free groceries. Kylie would provide the food, and she planned to do most of the cooking—if she could figure out that blasted stove.

With her cart piled high, she headed for checkout. The efficient cashier was too young to remember her. All to the good. Kylie wasn't in the mood to chat about the old days. All she wanted was to get out of here and get home. Maybe Henry or Muriel would have some idea where to get a tree.

By the time she'd loaded the back of the station wagon, a line of cars had formed behind the pickup driver who'd stopped to wait for her parking place. Horns were honking; tempers were flaring. Kylie did her best to hurry as she shut the tailgate and piled into the driver's seat. Only as she shifted into reverse and checked the side mirror did she see the problem. The pickup driver, a flustered-looking old man, had gone a few inches too far before stopping. If she backed straight out, her wagon would hit his front bumper.

With vehicles jammed in close behind him, there was no room for the old man to back up. The sensible thing would have been for him to drive ahead and give the spot to the next car. But either he hadn't thought of that or he wasn't willing to give up. He sat there with his hands on the wheel and his jaw set in a stubborn line.

The honking had risen to a clamoring din. Kylie willed herself to stay calm. Maybe if she swung the wagon's rear end hard to the right, she could back out of the parking space without hitting the truck.

Twisting the steering wheel, she eased down on the gas pedal. Hallelujah, it was working! The wagon inched backward, missing the truck's bumper by a finger's breadth. Sweating beneath her fleece jacket, she pulled out of the parking place. But she was still in trouble. Her vehicle was cross-blocking the way between two rows of parked cars. To get clear, she would need to make a sharp quarter-turn, and there was barely any room.

She steeled her nerves, checked her side mirrors and began a cautious backing-and-filling motion, working the car around in a counter-clockwise direction. Some of the waiting cars had begun to honk at her, but she was almost there. One more maneuver should do it. She couldn't wait to get out of this place and back on the road.

But she should have known this wasn't her lucky day. Backing up for the last time, she felt a slight bump of resistance. Then, from behind her wagon, she heard the awful crunch of twisting, folding metal.

Kylie's stomach lurched. She hit the brake and switched off the ignition. Legs shaking, she climbed out of the car. People had turned to look, but nobody was screaming or calling for the paramedics. It couldn't be too bad, she told herself. She'd barely been moving. If she'd caused a fender bender, her insurance would pay for it.

At first, she couldn't see what she'd hit. Then, as she walked around to the back of her vehicle, there it was. Her heart dropped.

Crumpled against the rear of her station wagon was the ruined front end of a vintage Harley-Davidson motorcycle.

Chapter Two

"You'd better get outside, Shane! Some damn-fool woman's backed into your bike!"

At the bag boy's words, Shane Taggart abandoned his cart in the coffee aisle and made a beeline for the front entrance of the store. *Not the bike,* a voice in his head shrilled. *Anything but the bike!*

Shane had owned the 1977 Harley-Davidson Low Rider since high school—so long that, when he rode it, the lovingly maintained machine felt like part of his body. Today he'd chosen to take it on one last run before draining the tank and locking it away for the winter. Bad decision. The idiot woman had probably been gabbing on her cell phone, not paying attention when she backed out of her parking place. Whoever she was, she was damn well going to pay.

Charging outside, he scanned the parking lot. A crowd had gathered around the spot where he'd parked the bike. Traffic was backing up. Angry drivers were yelling and blasting on their horns. Shane muttered a curse. Whatever was in the middle of that mess, it was bound to be bad.

Steeling himself, he strode across the parking lot. The knot of people clustered around the accident parted to let him through. Shane was well known in Branding Iron, and even the meanest of its citizens knew better than to mess with his motorcycle. They were no doubt expecting a showdown. Shane was of a mind to give them one.

He saw the bike first. Shane bit back a groan as he surveyed the crushed front wheel, the twisted forks, the broken gauges, and the cracked windscreen. Even if the frame wasn't bent, he'd have a major repair job on his hands—and genuine parts for a bike as old as this one were scarcer than diamonds and almost as pricey. He swore silently. Given a choice, he'd rather have broken his leg. At least bones could heal themselves.

"It was an accident. I'm sorry." The tremulous voice was smoky-sweet, like a swig of home-brewed peach brandy.

" 'Sorry'? Isn't it a little late for that?" Shane glowered down at her. She was petite, five-three at most, with short, strawberry blond curls and wide bluebonnet eyes. She wasn't a local—he'd have noticed her before now if she had been. Something about her did look vaguely familiar. But never mind. Experience had taught him that it was easier to be mad at a pretty woman than at a plain one. And he was mad as hell.

"Why didn't you look where you were going?" he growled. "Those rearview mirrors aren't just for putting on your lipstick."

Her posture stiffened. Her eyes flashed. "How can you say that? You don't even know what happened."

"I can see what happened." Shane knew he'd crossed a line, but he was in no mood to apologize. The vintage Harley had been his pride and joy. Now the front end of it was a twisted mess. He didn't even have a way back to his ranch.

"Fine," she snapped. "We can have a civilized conversation about this or you can deal with my insurance company. Your choice. Here's my card. If you want to copy the information, I can lend you a pen."

Shane took the printed yellow card and scanned it till his eyes found what he was looking for— her name.

KYLIE SUMMERFIELD WAYNE.

He felt a jarring sensation, like getting kicked in the rump by a steer. Shane bit back a curse. No wonder she'd looked familiar. He'd shared schoolrooms with snooty little Kylie Summerfield since the year they were in Miss Maccabee's kindergarten class.

"I'll be damned," he said.

Her blue eyes narrowed. "Nice to see you again, too, Shane."

Kylie had recognized him the moment he came charging out of the store. Shane Taggart, the town bad boy, who'd been suspended twice in ninth grade for smoking in the boys' lavatory. Shane Taggart who'd been tearing around on that motorcycle, with or without a license, since his legs got long enough to reach the foot pedals.

Now he loomed above her, all lean, hard six-foot-four of him. Warring emotions flickered across his movie-star face. Years of sun and wind had burnished his chiseled features like fine leather, deepening the set of his dark, hooded eyes and adding a glint of silver to the stubble that shadowed his jaw. Dressed in jeans, muddy cowboy boots, and a black leather jacket, he looked every inch the troublemaker he'd been in high school.

He had to be Aunt Muriel's so-called cowboy. No wonder he made her seventy-nine-year-old pulse flutter. Shane had always been a heart-breaker. One of the hearts he'd broken had been Kylie's—and he didn't even know it.

His gaze had returned to the smashed motor-cycle. Kylie recognized it now. It was the same machine he'd had as a teenage hellion. It looked meticulously cared for. Probably worth a lot of money now. Kylie had had enough experience with insurance companies to know they weren't inclined to pay much for vintage items. And on top of that, the sentimental value . . . Heaven save her, why hadn't she backed into something that could just be paid for and fixed—like maybe a brand-new BMW?

"I'll do anything I can to help," she said, trying to sound upbeat. "But first, we need a way out of this parking lot."

She eyed the worsening traffic snarl. The old man in the pickup had taken advantage of the melee to pull into the parking place and walk into the store, leaving Kylie trapped between the wrecked motorcycle and the honking cars, which were backed up in both directions. Shane surveyed the scene, taking silent measure. Then he went into action.

"Get in your car and stay there," he ordered her. Then he strode down the line of vehicles, talking to each of the drivers, barking instructions. Kylie couldn't hear what he was saying, but the sound of honking horns died into silence. At his signal, the cars began to back away slowly, out of the jammed parking lane. Within minutes the lane was clear.

Kylie was free to pull away and go. But she could hardly drive off and leave Shane stranded with a wrecked motorcycle.

She got out and walked around to the back. Shane was standing next to her rear bumper, scowling down at the wreck.

"It was amazing, the way you unsnarled that traffic jam," Kylie said.

He gave her a black look. "It's going to take a lot more than 'amazing' to fix this bike."

"Is there somewhere you can have it hauled?

My auto club membership should cover that, at least."

He shook his head. "This is no job for a body shop. It could take me weeks, even months to get parts, if I can get them at all. And I don't trust anybody to load and haul my bike but me. I'll need to hitch a ride back to the ranch and get my pickup."

"I can take you. I live out that way now."

One dark eyebrow lifted in silent question.

"We're staying with Aunt Muriel now—my two children and I. She told me you were her neighbor. But I hadn't planned on running into you so soon." Kylie's face went hot as she realized what she'd said. When she was a schoolgirl, being around Shane had always flustered her. But she'd never dreamed that effect would last into her thirties.

"If I'd known you were planning to run into me, I'd have stayed home." His mouth was smiling, but his eyes were as stormy as the dark clouds roiling across the sky. Kylie winced, catching the bitter edge in his tone.

"I didn't mean that literally," she said.

He turned away from her. "We're wasting time. Looks like the bike might be wedged under your bumper. Once I get it clear and moved out of the way, you can drive me home." He crouched to study the trapped front end of the bike. His hands manipulated the twisted parts—big hands, with long fingers—working hands, calloused and bruised. When she'd sat one desk away from him in American history class, Kylie had loved watching those hands—restless hands that moved and shifted as if he couldn't wait to be somewhere else.

He worked intently for a moment; then he twisted back to look at her. "Get in your car and start the engine. When I tell you, ease it forward till I say to stop."

Kylie climbed into the driver's seat, rolled down the windows, and started the engine. She could hear the scrape of metal at the rear of the station wagon. A snowflake drifted down onto her windshield, then another.

"Now," he said, "take it slow. That's it. . . . Stop."

Kylie touched the brake.

"Okay, it's clear," he said. "Give me some room now. Drive up to the loading lane at the front of the store and wait for me."

Kylie did as he'd asked. More snowflakes were falling now, drifting like eiderdown through the gray, windless air. Was this just a flurry or had the big storm already arrived?

The loading lane was a covered drive-up area, where shoppers, most of them elderly, could have their bags loaded into their cars. Kylie pulled into an out-of-the-way spot and turned on the radio.

". . . Looks like a white Christmas, folks, an honest-to-goodness blue norther. Snow's already coming down in some spots, but the big storm front's still out there. It's a slow mover, taking its time. But when it gets here, we'll be up past our knees in white stuff. You ranchers know to look out for your stock. The rest of you, get your pets under cover and don't plan to be out on the roads. . . ."

Glancing out the side window, she saw one of the baggers from the store, a husky teen, helping Shane support the bike like a wounded comrade as they wheeled it toward the covered area. They parked it out of sight behind a Dumpster. When Kylie pulled forward, she could hear the two of them talking through her lowered window.

"Don't worry, Shane, I'll keep an eye on it," the boy was saying. "Nobody will touch your bike while I'm around."

"Make sure." Shane slipped him a bill. "I'll be back to pick it up in an hour."

Kylie braced herself as he turned and walked back to her car. She owed Shane a ride to his ranch and plenty more for wrecking his precious motorcycle. And she had little doubt he'd collect his due—starting now.

With a last glance at his battered bike, Shane slid into the passenger seat of the station wagon. The vehicle looked like it had seen better days. But as for the driver—Kylie looked damn good. Older, wiser, and sexier than the perfect, untouchable girl he remembered from high school.

"I heard what you told that boy. You could be driving through a blizzard in an hour," she said.

"Wouldn't be the first time." He fastened his seat belt, gazing out the window as Kylie headed for the road. Part of him wanted to rail at her for the careless maneuver that had destroyed his bike. But behaving like a jackass wouldn't fix anything. "So you're staying at Muriel's—with two kids. There's got to be a story behind that."

"Nothing that interesting." Kylie switched on her wipers as snowflakes settled on the windshield. "My husband was a captain in the army. He was killed in Afghanistan nineteen months ago. This fall, after our house in California got foreclosed, Muriel offered us a home in exchange for some help around the place. We just got in yesterday."

"California, huh?" He rubbed the stubble on his chin. "The move out here's bound to be an adjustment for your kids. How old are they?"

"Eleven and thirteen. And no . . . they're not happy about the change. But I don't know what we'd have done if Aunt Muriel hadn't invited us to come here. I tried to find a job in San Diego. But being an ex–army wife isn't exactly a marketable skill."

He studied her profile, the pert nose, the pink,

girlish lips, the tired shadows beneath her baby blue eyes. She'd had a rough time of it, losing her husband and dealing with two kids on the verge of adolescence. But that was no excuse for causing a stupid accident that could've been prevented by a touch on the brake. He would have to keep reminding himself of that.

"What about you?" A nervous hand brushed back her short, tousled hair. She still wore her wedding ring, he noticed. "As I remember, all you wanted was to get out of Branding Iron and bike your way to the tip of South America. You even took that awful Spanish class to help you get ready," she said.

"Only class I got a decent grade in. I can't believe you remembered that."

"I remember a lot of things. Did you ever make the trip?"

He shook his head, still feeling the sting of memory. "My father had a stroke. I couldn't leave him to run the ranch alone."

"So you've been here all this time."

"At least I've still got the bike—or did have it until today."

Her jaw tightened. She didn't reply. At least maybe she understood now that the accident had shattered his long-held dream, or at least put it on hold. When he was growing up, all he'd wanted was to roam the world on that old bike. He'd seen the movie *The Motorcycle Diaries* more times than he could count, and he'd worn out his copies of Jack Kerouac's *On the Road* and Robert Pirsig's *Zen and the Art of Motorcycle Maintenance.* The last thing he'd wanted was to be stuck in Branding Iron, Texas, for the rest of his life. But day by day, the years had passed, and here he was.

By now, snow was flying at the windshield in big, silent flakes to be whisked away by the wipers. Beyond the car, the fields of yellowed grass were already dusted with white. A rider in a field was herding cows toward shelter. From the radio, the sounds of Christmas music tugged at the fringes of Shane's memory. When he was a little boy, his mother had made Christmas a magical time. After her early death from cancer, Shane's father had refused to celebrate the holiday. Now that he, too, was gone, Shane saw no reason to change things.

"Is your father still alive?" Kylie asked.

"He died last year. I'll be putting the ranch up for sale this spring."

"So you'll get the chance to travel, after all."

"Maybe not South America, but I'd like to see most of the USA, maybe Canada, by the back roads. At least that's the plan." *Or was the plan.* Shane bit back the words. Kylie was well aware of what she'd done. Of course, if he sold the ranch, he could afford to buy a new high-end motorcycle. But that old bike was a lifelong friend; the trip he'd planned a promise kept—a silly, sentimental idea, Shane knew. But he'd felt that way for too many years to give in to cold logic.

"So, did you ever get married? Any children?"

Shane forced himself to laugh. "Met a couple of ladies who got me thinking about it, but that's as far as it went. Just not sure I'm husband-and-father material." He glanced at the gold wedding band on her finger. "I take it you had better luck."

She hesitated and he heard the little catch in her throat. "Brad was a fine man, and I loved him. But the army kept him away for months at a time. I learned early on to cope with everyday challenges on my own. But now that I know he's not coming back . . ." Her voice trailed into silence. She was probably thinking she'd told him too much.

Maybe she had.

The drive from town wasn't a long one. Through the falling snow, he could see the turnoff to his ranch, and beyond that, the gate and the house and barns. Eight hundred acres wasn't big by Texas standards, but it had been Taggart land since Shane's great-grandfather had bought the parcel at Depression-era prices and built the spacious stone house that Shane now rattled around in alone. Even after all these years, the house was imposing, with two stately pines flanking the broad front porch. The soil was rich, the grass abundant, with plenty of well water under the ground. Shane had seen to it that the hay fields were well fertilized, and the pens and outbuildings kept in good repair. Somebody was bound to want the place and pay a good price for it.

Then he'd be free.

By the time Kylie pulled up to the shed where Shane kept his truck, snow was crunching under the tires. Shane hadn't been unpleasant, but she'd felt his frustration and known she was the cause of it. The tension between them had been thick enough to give her a headache.

"Thanks for the ride." She could feel the edge in his voice.

"You're welcome. My number's on the card I gave you. Call me when you want to talk about the insurance."

"Sure."

"Aunt Muriel told me you come around to help, so I guess we'll be seeing each other, now and then."

"Yeah, I guess." He paused. "You can tell Henry I'll be dropping the bike off tonight. If the weather's not too bad, I'll be back in the morning to see what he thinks about fixing it."

Kylie had started to pull away. Her foot hit the brake. "Wait, you're saying you'll be leaving the motorcycle at our place?"

"That's what I said. Henry Samuels has the

best-equipped machine shop in the county. If anybody can help me fix the bike, he can."

Shane watched the station wagon vanish into the flying snow. Then he turned and sprinted toward the barn. He needed to get back on the road to pick up the bike. But he made it a rule not to leave until he checked on the animals.

The Taggart ranch was a haying-and-feeder operation: buying young steers in the spring, putting weight on them for a long season, then selling the grass-fed Anguses at a premium in late fall. Shane had auctioned the last of the herd and paid off his temporary help a few weeks earlier, so there were no cattle in the snowy fields. But he had to make sure the ranch's permanent residents were safe in the barn, with plenty of food and water in case the storm delayed his getting home.

The warm barn smelled of hay and animals. Gray light fell through the high windows below the roof, but the place was still dark. Shane switched on the electric light, reminding himself to check the fuel in the reserve generator before he left.

The half-dozen chickens that ran loose around the place were settled in the straw or pecking at the grain he'd tossed on the floor. The three horses stood drowsing in their stalls. Shane forked extra hay into their feeders and filled their water troughs from the hose.

Inside the fourth stall, Shane had set up a high-sided box to contain the four puppies that were romping in the clean straw, tumbling over their patient mother. They were blue heelers—registered Australian cattle dogs with dark blue markings and beautiful blue-ticked coats, the finest animals on earth for working cattle.

Shane had been breeding and selling the pups as a sideline for the past eight years. It had started when he'd bought Mick, the big, intelligent male who'd become his constant companion. Mick had even learned to perch on the back of Shane's motorcycle when they rode into town. When other ranchers had expressed interest in owning such a dog, Shane had bought Sheila, a sharp young female with champion bloodlines, and began breeding them.

There was a waiting list for pups. Three of these were already spoken for. But this litter would be the last. Mick had died last fall at the age of fourteen. A breeder had offered Shane five thousand dollars for Sheila, but she was getting old, too, and Shane wanted a better future for her than a breeding kennel. Once these pups were weaned, he planned to take Sheila to the vet and have her spayed. Carl, the bagger at Shop Mart who worked summers for Shane, was waiting to give her a good home.

Outside the box, Shane filled Sheila's bowl to the rim with kibble and gave her plenty of water.

For her pups, he filled a low tray with puppy chow and put it in one corner. They scrambled to crunch it with their baby teeth. Now that they were eating solid food, their mother would be ready for a well-earned rest.

Leaning over the box, he scratched Sheila's ears. She thumped her tail in response. She was a beautiful dog, sweet and spirited. Carl loved her and would take good care of her.

The puppies had scattered their chow in the straw and were sniffing for the pieces. Shane scooped up the only male of the four—the pup he'd decided to keep for himself. Mick Junior— "Mickey" would be his nickname—was a carbon copy of his father, with the same perfect markings and eager disposition. Mick's last son. Shane couldn't look at the sharp-nosed baby face without feeling a tug at his heart. "So, boy, do you think you can learn to ride a motorcycle like your old man?" he asked.

His own question slammed Shane with the reality of the accident. It was still sinking in how serious the damage was and how it could change his plans. Rotten luck that he'd taken his precious motorcycle to town today—and parked it right where Kylie Summerfield—no, Kylie Wayne— would back into it. He was still angry—partly at her, but mostly at himself.

Never mind, he could brood about that later. Right now, he needed to get his truck back to town and pick up the bike while the roads were still drivable.

Shane put the pup down next to the mother, closed the barn door, and strode across the yard through the flying snow.

By the time Shane neared town, the roads were caked with slippery snow. Longtime residents who'd been through these storms before knew enough to slow down and to tap the brake pedal lightly instead of slamming it and sending their tires into a skid. Newcomers, who hadn't learned to drive on icy roads, were sliding and spinning like Olympic figure skaters. Between the city limits and the Shop Mart parking lot, Shane was nearly hit twice. Skillful dodging saved his truck from being bashed, but he was sweating under his coat as he pulled up to Shop Mart. One wreck was enough for the day.

The sheriff's big tan SUV was parked next to the Dumpster, where Shane had left his wrecked bike. Sheriff Ben Marsden was standing under the overhang of the storefront, as if waiting for him. Somebody must've called the accident in.

Ben glanced around as Shane climbed out of the pickup. He was tall, with piercing gray eyes beneath his felt trooper hat. His body had filled out some since he was all-state quarterback in high school. But the man was still rock-hard and Texas tough. Nobody messed with Ben Marsden.

He and Shane hadn't been friends in their school years. Ben had been the all-American boy, Shane the rebel. But they'd long since outgrown those days and settled their differences. The two men liked and respected each other.

Ben glanced back at the bike. "Tough break, Shane. I know what that old bike meant to you."

"Yeah. Merry Christmas." Shane spoke the words with a twist of irony.

"Carl, here—" He nodded toward the bagboy. "He told me some woman backed into your bike while it was parked. I was wondering if you wanted to fill out an accident report and press charges."

Shane shook his head. "It happened on private property, and she wasn't doing anything illegal. Just trying to back out of a bad spot. I was mad as hell, still am. But punishing her won't fix the bike."

"She's got insurance?"

Shane nodded. "She offered to pay. But the insurance money I'd get for that old bike might not be worth the bother."

"Well, that's your decision." Ben stared out across the parking lot, where the cars were already buried under a layer of white. "Rumor has it, you're planning to saddle up and leave town."

"That's right. Got my ranch listed for sale. Want to buy it?"

Ben's chuckle carried an edge. "Wish I could.

But it's all I can do to manage alimony and child support. Cheryl's got me over a barrel."

Ben had married the homecoming queen he'd met in college. It had turned out to be a bad idea. "See much of your boy these days?" Shane asked. "Sorry, I forget his name."

"It's Joshua. And no, I don't see him near enough. Now that he's five and in school, the visits are even harder to schedule, especially with his mother pulling the strings." He glanced back toward the bike. "I guess things are tough all over. C'mon, let me help you load your machine so you can get the hell out of here."

Carl had been called back inside. Shane rigged a single ramp, and together the two men wheeled the crippled bike into the back of the pickup truck and laid in the loose pieces. Shane threw a canvas tarp over it to keep off the snow and climbed into the driver's seat.

Ben motioned to Shane as he was about to start the engine. Shane rolled down the window. "I forgot to ask," Ben said. "Did you get some I.D. on the woman who hit your bike?"

"I recognized her when she gave me her card," Shane said. "Remember Kylie Summerfield from school?"

"Kylie? I'll be damned. Sure, I remember her. Nice girl. A little too goody-goody for my taste, but pretty—and smart. So she's back in town. What's her story?"

"Widowed, down on her luck. She and her two kids have moved in with Muriel. She's as good-looking as ever. You might want to check her out. Hey, maybe you could ask her about the accident."

Ben chuckled and shook his head. "The last thing I need right now is another woman in my life. My mother had a nasty fall in her old house yesterday. I'm planning to move back in after the holidays, just so somebody will be there. At least it'll save me rent and give me a good place for Joshua when he shows up. Anyway, I get the feeling you're the one who's interested in Kylie."

"Not me, especially since the lady's still wearing her wedding ring."

"You could fix that. Good luck with the bike." Ben thumped twice on the top of the cab, a sign for Shane to move on. Shane started the engine and pulled carefully out of the parking lot. The snow was getting heavier. He turned on the wipers and the defroster. With the roads so bad, Ben was going to have a busy night. He could only hope none of the accidents would be serious.

Why had he suggested that his friend check out Kylie? Ben was a good man. But truth be told, despite her wrecking his bike, Shane found Kylie intriguingly sexy. Was he worried about getting involved with her when he was about to leave town? Was he trying to protect himself from the stirrings he'd felt when he was in the car with her? Was that why he'd tried to steer Ben in her direction?

But never mind that. He had more pressing worries on his mind—like getting home in this storm and repairing the bike Kylie had smashed. With snow pelting down so thick he could barely see the road, and the tires barely gripping the surface, he'd be smart to keep his mind off Kylie and on his driving.

Chapter Three

Kylie pulled her station wagon up to the house and trudged, head down, through the flying snow to unload the groceries from the back. The main storm front was blowing in, its icy winds plastering her thin fleece jacket to her body. She shivered as she raised the tailgate. Her hands trembled, and not just from the cold. The accident had left her rattled—and her head was still spinning from her encounter with Shane Taggart.

Shane Taggart, of all people. And judging from the look of that bike, and the look on his gorgeously handsome face, she'd come close to ruining his life.

"Mom, where's the Christmas tree? Didn't you get one?" Flinging open the door, Amy rushed down the front steps, followed by her brother.

Kylie shook her head. "Sorry, they were sold out in town. But I haven't given up. Here, take these bags and run them inside."

"Who cares about a dumb old Christmas tree, anyway? Christmas is for spoiled babies." Hunter dragged an armful of grocery bags out of the wagon. Both Kylie's children were wearing light jackets, the warmest wraps they'd needed in San Diego. Online she'd ordered winter coats, boots, and gloves to be delivered here, along with the Christmas presents. At the time she'd congratulated herself for planning ahead. But now here she was with her children, stuck in a blizzard with nothing warm to wear. They would have to dress in layers until the packages arrived. When she could spare a minute, she would use her phone to check the shipment status. The shipper had guaranteed Christmas delivery. That meant a sure thing, didn't it?

"Get inside before you freeze, girl." Henry had come around the corner of the house; he was wearing work boots and a military-style parka, with the hood drawn tight around his face. "Give me your keys. I'll put the car under the shed for you."

"Th—thanks!" Kylie's teeth were chattering. She grabbed the last grocery bag, closed the tailgate, and dropped the keys into Henry's hand. The porch steps were slippery with snow.

She couldn't help wondering how Shane was

faring on the roads. But his truck would have four-wheel drive, and he'd lived around Branding Iron all his life. He'd know how to handle bad weather.

Still, anything that might happen to him would be her fault. If she hadn't hit his motorcycle, he'd have made it safely home before snow covered the roads.

The house smelled of the savory beef stew that simmered on the stove. Kylie knew her children wouldn't care for stew. Burgers and pizza would be their choice. But she'd already made it clear to them—one word of complaint about the food and they'd be sent straight to their rooms.

Henry stomped the snow off his boots and came in the kitchen door to give her the key. When Kylie thanked him, he responded with a muttered "You're welcome." With his parka hood pulled back, he was a handsome old man, with thick, white hair and a strong, square jaw. Always polite and helpful, he'd worked for Muriel's late father. Kylie remembered him from when she was a little girl. But he was a private man, reserved to the point of shyness; even after so many years, he was hard to know well.

"You'll stay for supper, won't you, Henry?" Muriel glanced up from stirring the stew. "There's fresh biscuits in the oven."

He hesitated. "Sure you'll have enough? Shane called. He's bringin' his bike by to leave in the machine shed for some bodywork. He's liable to be hungry, too."

"Leaving his bike?" Muriel's eyes widened. "Mercy, what happened to it?"

"Seems some fool woman ran into it at Shop Mart and busted the whole front end. Shane sounded pretty sore about it."

Unloading grocery bags on the counter, Kylie felt her stomach lurch. A plastic milk jug slipped out of her hand and crashed to the floor. She crouched to pick it up, checking the jug for leaks and, luckily, finding none. Maybe Shane was giving her a break. At least he hadn't told Henry who the "fool woman" had been. Or maybe he had, and it was Henry who was keeping her secret.

Should she fess up? She glanced at her children. Amy was helping set the table. Hunter was sitting on a stool in the corner, texting on his phone. Kylie had always tried to set a good example for them. What if one of them had caused an accident? What would she want them to do?

There was only one right answer to that question.

She finished putting the milk in the fridge. Muriel had gone back to stirring the stew. Henry was lingering by the back door, as if uncertain whether to go or stay.

She cleared her throat, scrambling for a way to begin. "Henry, did Shane tell you anything about the woman who wrecked his bike?" she asked.

Henry shook his head. "He called her 'addle-brained.' But he didn't say who she was."

Kylie straightened her spine, squared her jaw and took a deep breath. "In that case, I have a confession to make. The 'addle-brained fool woman' who ran into Shane's motorcycle was . . . me."

"Oh, dear!" Muriel's spoon slid into the stew and sank beneath the bubbling surface. Henry's jaw dropped in speechless dismay.

"It was an accident." Kylie was talking fast now, rushing the words. "The parking lot was a mess. I'd just backed out of my space, but there wasn't room to straighten the car and drive away. I was maneuvering when I backed too far and hit the bike in the next row behind me." She paused for breath. "Did Shane tell you I drove him home, and that I said my insurance would pay for it?"

"Can't say he took the time for that," Henry muttered, shaking his head.

"Goodness, dear." Muriel looked stunned. "I can't imagine why someone used to driving in California would have so much trouble driving here."

Kylie glanced at her children. Hunter was still texting, as if he hadn't heard. But Amy stood there, clasping a handful of cutlery, with an indignant look on her face. "Aunt Muriel," she said, "it just so happens we don't have snow in

San Diego. And we don't have Texas drivers, either."

For the space of a breath, there was silence in the kitchen. Then Henry chuckled, breaking the tension. "Good for you, young lady. I like a girl who sticks up for her mother."

Kylie would have crossed the room and hugged her daughter, but just then a ferocious gust of wind shook the house, battering the windows and blasting the panes with snow. Above the storm's howl, they heard the sound of a honking horn and a truck pulling into the backyard. "That'll be Shane." Henry raised the hood on his parka and started for the door. "He'll need me to give him a hand."

"Bring him back inside," Muriel called after him. "And you come, too, Henry. There's plenty of food."

By now, it was getting dark outside. As Henry stepped onto the back porch, a gust of wind almost knocked him over. The door blew out of his hand and slammed back hard against the kitchen wall. Stinging, ice-flecked air rushed into the kitchen. Kylie sprinted across the room to shove the door closed. "Good grief!" she exclaimed. "I hope this storm blows through fast. We still need to get a tree from somewhere before Christmas."

"There should be one of those old flocked-silver trees in the attic." Muriel was using salad tongs to fish the dropped spoon out of the stew. "I haven't bothered with a tree in years, but you're welcome to use it. Maybe Hunter can haul it down for us."

"No!" Amy had sounded so grown-up a moment ago. Now she was pouting like a little girl. "Those old fake trees are hideous! You said we could have a *real* tree, Mom. You *promised!*"

"Yes, I did. And I haven't given up." Kylie sighed. She'd vowed to give her children a good Christmas, and that included a fresh pine tree with her family's treasured decorations on its fragrant boughs and beautifully wrapped presents piled underneath. Why should that be so hard? Why, for once, couldn't doing something good for her children be easy?

So help her, she would get a real tree for Christmas, even if she had to borrow a saw, wade through the snow, and cut one down herself!

Muriel had rescued the spoon and was rinsing it off in the sink. "I still can't believe you had the bad luck to wreck the cowboy's motorcycle," she said. "Was he mad?"

Kylie shuddered. "He was livid. After we discovered we knew each other, he did his best to calm down. But according to Henry, he's still angry—and I can't say I blame him. I ruined one of his most precious possessions."

"You say you knew each other?"

"That's right. We went through school together,

all the way from kindergarten to twelfth grade. Shane was always skating the edge of trouble. In high school, I remember him ditching class to go roaring off on that old bike." And she remembered how she'd ached to ride behind him, her arms around his waist, holding him tight as her hair bannered behind her in the wind. Sometimes he took girls on his bike—girls who were reputed to be wild and fast. But he never took her.

"You were valedictorian, as I recall," Muriel said.

"And Shane managed to graduate by the skin of his teeth. He was smart as a whip, but he was bored with school. All he wanted was to get out of Branding Iron and see the world." Kylie carried two extra bowls and plates to the table for the men. With Shane there, she wouldn't have much of an appetite, but she owed it to Muriel to put on a good face.

"Knowing how much he wanted to leave, I was surprised to see Shane was still in town," she said.

Muriel lifted the pot of stew off the hot burner. "Well, dear, sometimes family duty trumps selfish wishes. He's done a fine job of running the ranch for his father all these years."

Kylie wanted to bite her tongue. Shane and Muriel had made similar sacrifices—giving up whatever dreams they'd had to stay home and carry on for ailing parents. Who was she to sit in judgment?

The sound of boots stamping off snow on the back porch broke into the conversation. The door opened far enough to admit Henry, then Shane, who was gripping the knob to keep the wind from blasting it out of his hand. Wrapped in a thick sheepskin coat with the collar turned up to his ears, snowflakes glimmering in his dark, tousled hair, his face ruddy from the cold . . . Kylie stifled a groan. Muriel's cowboy neighbor looked as delectable as a hot-fudge sundae with sprinkles.

She was long since over Shane, of course. He'd been nothing more than a one-sided high-school crush. But heaven help her, the man was still an eyeful!

Tearing her gaze away, she moved the stew pot off the stove and ladled the stew into a big serving bowl. It looked and smelled delicious, but Amy and Hunter were already rolling their eyes and wrinkling their noses. If her finicky children hurt Muriel's feelings, there would be words later on.

After Shane was introduced to Kylie's children, he and Henry hung their damp coats over the backs of the chairs and went to the half bath off the kitchen to wash up. By the time they came back, the meal was on the table, ready to eat.

"Thanks, Muriel." Shane took his seat, his tall frame dwarfing the small, crowded kitchen table.

"I've been hankering for some of your beef stew and biscuits. Just right for a cold night like this."

Muriel flushed at his praise. "Same old thing I've always made," she said. "Eat up. There's plenty."

Hunter was reaching for a hot, golden biscuit when Henry stopped him with a stern look. "Wait till we've said grace, young man."

Hunter and Amy looked startled. Brad hadn't been a religious man, and their eat-and-run California lifestyle hadn't included a prayer before meals. One more thing that would take some getting used to.

"Would you say it, please, Henry?" Muriel asked.

Henry nodded. As he bowed his head, Muriel reached out to join hands with the children, who sat on either side of her. Unused to the custom, but sensing they should follow along, Amy and Hunter reached for the hands on either side— Henry's and Shane's. Kylie had taken the last empty chair, between the two men. One hand slipped lightly into Henry's work-roughened palm. Her other reached toward Shane.

Their fingers brushed and fumbled. Then his big, leathery hand, still chilled from the cold, closed around hers. Tingles of awareness swept through her body. After all the teenage fantasies that had begun with Shane taking her hand, she'd never expected it to happen under these circumstances. The contact of skin to skin sent her pulse skittering. This was crazy. She was a grown woman, a widow with children, not a silly schoolgirl.

Henry's mumbled prayer was mercifully brief. As the hushed "amen" echoed around the table, Shane's clasp loosened and Kylie pulled her still-tingling hand away. Amy and Hunter were already grabbing for the fluffy golden biscuits, ignoring the stew Muriel had ladled into their bowls. A lesson in manners would be in order before the next meal.

"That's more than your share, Hunter," she admonished her son as he reached for a third biscuit. "Leave enough for the others. If you're hungry, eat more of this delicious stew."

Hunter poked at a carrot slice with his spoon, wrinkled his nose, then lifted a small chunk of beef to his mouth and chewed it as if he expected some kind of trick. "Not too bad," he pronounced.

" 'Not too bad'?" Shane raised an eyebrow. "If you ask me, Muriel's the best darned cook in the county. Isn't she, Henry?"

"Far as I know." Henry bit into a buttered biscuit.

"I'm hoping she'll give me a few lessons," Kylie said. "I've got a lot to learn about that temperamental old stove."

"Once you know what to expect from it, you'll be fine, dear." Muriel glanced around the table.

"Cowboy, I was so sorry to hear about your motorcycle. I know you loved that old bike."

"Can't undo what happened." Shane's face was a stoic mask. "All we can do is try to fix it."

"And what if it can't be fixed?" Muriel persisted, heedless of Kylie's unease.

He shrugged. "Nothing lasts forever. Guess I'll cross that bridge when I come to it."

Kylie shrank in her chair. All she wanted right now was to slide under the table and disappear. But she had no choice except to sit here and endure the cold anger that radiated from Shane's powerful body—the anger he couldn't quite manage to hide.

They ate in silence for a few moments; the children were picking the meat out of the stew and leaving the vegetables, Shane spooning up his stew as if he couldn't wait to finish and leave. Outside, the howling storm battered the windows.

"How were the roads, Shane?" Kylie spoke into the awkward hush. "Did you have any trouble getting back from town?"

"It was tough going after the front came in. But as you can see, I made it this far. So I guess I can make it home from here. Mighty grateful for the good supper, Muriel." He pushed back his chair and stood. Tired shadows framed his dark eyes. "Guess I'd better be on my way."

"Wait!" Amy hadn't said a word during the

meal, but now she almost jumped out of her chair. "You might know this. Where can we get a real Christmas tree around here? Is there a farm or someplace that sells them—or a forest, where we can go cut one down?"

Shane ran a hand through his damp hair. A weary look passed across his face. Kylie sensed that all he really wanted was to get out of here and get home. But at least he seemed to be thinking about his answer.

"I'll check around," he said. "But nothing's going to happen till this storm clears, so don't get your hopes up. Okay?"

Amy's expression drooped. "Okay. But do you promise you'll check?"

"If there's anything to check." He shrugged into his sheepskin coat and fastened a couple of buttons. "I'll be back in the morning to start on the bike, Henry. Thanks again."

"Be careful going home," Henry said. "It's bad out there. You could freeze if you get stuck in that storm."

"Don't worry, I'll be fine." Shane turned up his collar; then he opened the door and forced it shut as he stepped into the wind.

Shane trudged head forward, pushing his way through blinding snow that was already deep enough to fall inside his boot tops. The roads would be a mess tonight, but they'd be even worse later on. If he was going to be snowed in somewhere, he needed to be home.

He'd left the truck under the overhang of the shed, where it would be protected from the worst of the storm. But as he battled his way across the yard, he realized he was moving by rote, finding his way only because he knew it so well. In the snow-filled dark, he could barely see his hand in front of his face.

He ran into the truck almost before he saw it. But once he'd moved under the overhanging roof, his vision cleared some. The snow on the sheltered windows needed only a light brushing to clear them before he climbed inside, shifted gears, and started the engine. The truck swung out of the shed, grinding forward a dozen feet before it lost momentum and stopped, wheels spinning in the snow.

He was stuck. And even if he could go forward, there was no way he'd be able to find the road. The truck's headlights reflected on a wall of swirling snowflakes. Whether he liked it or not, the only safe place to go was back inside the house—with Kylie Summerfield Wayne and her two sullen, prepubescent kids. He climbed out of the truck and closed the door. It was going to be a long night.

The storm's howl had risen to a shriek. Snow-flakes spattered like buckshot against the house.

Peering through the window toward the lane that led to the road, Kylie watched for the red taillights of Shane's departing truck. But as the minutes crawled past, she could see nothing except the white blur of driving snow against the dark.

"I don't like this," she murmured, half to herself.

"I don't, either." Henry stood behind her. "There's no way he's going to get home in this. Got a flashlight, Muriel?"

"Right here." Muriel, who'd been clearing the table, opened a drawer and passed him the flashlight she found. Henry turned it on and checked the brightness. He'd just started for the door when it flew open and would've crashed against the wall if Henry hadn't stopped it. Shane staggered inside, his hair and coat layered with snow.

"Total whiteout, and it's getting deeper by the minute." Even the stubble along his jaw was coated. "I made it halfway across the yard and had to leave the truck because I couldn't see past the front bumper. Sorry, Muriel, but it looks like I'll have to stick around till it clears. If you've got a rag or a handy mop, I'll soak up the snowmelt."

His coat was already steaming in the warm kitchen. He hung it over the back of a chair, caught the old towel Muriel tossed him, and laid it on the floor to catch the dripping snow.

"No way you'll be getting out of here till morning, Cowboy," Muriel said. "You might as well plan to spend the night."

Kylie did some fast thinking. The four-bedroom house would've had plenty of room for a guest before she showed up with Hunter and Amy. Now the rooms were full, and Henry's small trailer had only one bed.

"Shane can have my room," she said. "I'll share with Amy for the night."

"I won't put you out." Shane sank onto a kitchen chair and began working off his wet cowboy boots. "I'll just crash on the couch for a few hours. That way, if the storm lets up in the night, I can leave and not bother a soul. I've got animals to tend, and I need to make sure the pipes won't freeze in the house. I'll be needing to get home."

"If that's what you really want, I'll get you a quilt and a pillow," Muriel said.

"We can't go to bed yet!" Amy turned away from stacking the dishes in the sink. "My TV show starts at eight. Can I watch it, Mom? See, I've been helping."

Amy's favorite TV show, about two teen girls solving crimes, was one of the few things she still had to look forward to. "Is it all right?" Kylie glanced at Muriel.

"Of course, dear. Maybe I'll watch it, too," Muriel said.

"Stupid show." Hunter glanced up from his phone. "Stupid baby show."

"It is not!" Amy turned on him. "It's better than those dumb video games you play."

"I can't play them here! I can't do anything here! And I don't have any friends! I hate this place!"

"That's enough, Hunter." Kylie was on her feet, snatching the phone out of his hand. "We'll talk about your getting this back after you've washed the dishes."

"That's not fair!" Hunter stormed. "I never had to wash dishes back home."

"That's because we had a dishwasher. But this is a different place and we all need to help out. Now get moving!"

Scowling, Hunter shuffled to the sink and began running hot water into the dishpan. Muriel stood by to give him a few pointers. Henry, still standing near the door in his coat, shuffled his feet.

"Well, since I planned to watch the basketball game, I'll be going," he said. "Come watch it with me if you want, Shane. I've got beer in the fridge."

Kylie saw Shane hesitate. "Thanks, Henry. I'd enjoy that, but with that storm out there and no place to sleep in your trailer, I'd better stay put." He stood. "I'll come out on the porch to see that you make it across the yard. Take the flashlight and wave it when you get to your door. That way I'll know you're safe."

Standing on the back porch in his stocking feet, Shane peered through the flying snow and watched the thin beam of light bob across the yard. Shivering, he counted the seconds until the light waved back and forth, signaling that Henry had made it to his trailer. Holy Hannah, but it was cold!

He would've enjoyed watching the game and sharing a beer with the old man. But the cramped space in Henry's trailer left little room to stretch out. And he'd be leaving two women and two kids alone during a dangerous storm. Staying in the house was the only choice that made sense.

Gripping the door to keep it from blowing open, he slipped back inside. Kylie was standing by the table, almost as if she'd been waiting for him.

"My word, you look like a human icicle!" she said.

"I f-feel like one, too." His teeth were chattering.

Kylie laughed—the first he'd heard her laugh since they were in school together. He'd forgotten how much he used to like that sound.

Back then, he'd liked a lot of things about Kylie Summerfield. She was pretty, she was smart, and she was nice to everybody. But she was the perfect girl—perfect looks, perfect clothes, perfect grades, perfect reputation—a girl who wouldn't be caught dead with a trouble-making loser like him.

So he'd stayed away. And he'd be smart to stay away now.

Her hand brushed his arm. "You're freezing! Aunt Muriel, where can I get a blanket?"

"Try the hall closet," Muriel called from the living room, where she'd gone to sit with Amy.

Kylie flitted away and came back with a woolen Indian-style blanket, which she unfolded and wrapped over his shoulders. Shane tugged its warmth around him.

"Can I make you something hot?" she asked. "Some cocoa?"

"Sounds good."

"I'll take some, too," Amy called from the living room. "How about you, Aunt Muriel?"

"You bet," Muriel said.

"Me too." Hunter had finished the dishes.

"Okay! Cocoa for everybody. We've even got marshmallows."

Wrapped in the blanket, Shane sat and watched as she gathered her supplies and began heating the cocoa. There was something cozy about sitting here, watching a pretty woman make something good. Kylie had changed since high school, he thought. She was softer, warmer—and sexy, damn it. Sexy in a way the perfect girl he remembered hadn't been.

Too bad he wasn't in the market. Now that he had the chance to leave Branding Iron forever, the last thing he wanted was to get tied down in a relationship, especially with kids involved.

"Mom?" Hunter stood beside her. "Can I have my phone back now?"

She took the phone out of her pocket. "Here. But remember to behave yourself. If I have to take it again, it'll be for longer."

"I'll remember!" He snatched the phone, turned it on, and began texting, his fingers a blur.

Kylie set out five mismatched mugs and dropped a marshmallow into each one. When the cocoa was hot, she filled the cups, set one down on the table next to Shane, handed one to Hunter, and put the rest on a tray.

"Thanks." He sipped the hot chocolate, tasting the marshmallow foam on his lips. He could hear the TV from the living room. Kylie walked through the open archway to set the tray on the coffee table. He found himself hoping she'd come back to the kitchen and keep him company, but she settled herself on the couch, next to her daughter, to watch the show. His only companion in the kitchen was Hunter, so absorbed in his phone that he might as well have been a robot.

The storm was a real blue norther, and it wasn't letting up. Wind clawed at the siding on the house. Snow hammered the windowpanes. Lulled by the sweet, hot cocoa, Shane was growing drowsy when, suddenly, from somewhere outside, there was a flash and a boom.

The lights flickered and went out, plunging the house and everyone in it into blackness.

Chapter Four

"Oh no!" The wail came from the living room. Shane recognized the tween-age voice of Kylie's daughter, Amy. "This isn't fair! It was just getting good!"

Shane pushed to his feet, leaving the blanket on the chair. "Is everybody all right in there?"

"No!" It was Amy again. "It's not fair! I want to watch my show!"

"Stop being a baby!" Hunter spoke from a dark corner of the kitchen. "The power went out, that's all. Who cares if you can't watch your stupid show? Hey, at least my phone still works!"

"Mom!"

"That's enough, both of you. If you can't be helpful, be quiet," Kylie said. "We're fine, Shane. Just sitting here in the dark. Any idea what happened?"

"There's a transformer on a pole by the road. I'm guessing it shorted out, maybe blew over, or even got hit by lightning. If that's what happened, we could be down till the power company makes it through the snow. Have you got a handy flashlight, Muriel?"

"Just the one we lent Henry," Muriel said. "Maybe you ought to call him and make sure he's all right."

"Good idea." Shane had the number of Henry's landline on his cell. The old man answered on the first ring.

"I'm fine," Henry said. "Since I'm the one with the good flashlight, do you want me to go out to the shed and try to crank up the generator? It hasn't been run for a while. Might need some fresh gas and some tinkerin'."

"No, stay put. I'll help you in the morning when it's light enough to see what we're doing. We'll be fine till then. Just stay safe and keep warm."

Shane ended the call. By now, his eyes were getting used to the dark. He could see the outlines of windows and furniture and the huddled shape that was the boy in the far corner of the kitchen. "Any candles?" he asked Muriel.

"Hall closet, bottom shelf," she answered from the living room. "I can come and—"

"No, I'll find them." The last thing Shane wanted was to have a seventy-nine-year-old woman stumble and break a bone. He made his way down the pitch-dark hallway; he found the closet and groped along the low shelf until his fingers closed on a bundle of tapered candles bound with a rubber band.

Holding the candles, he straightened, turned, and stepped out of the closet—only to bump into something soft, warm, and womanly. Even in the dark, there was no mistaking Kylie's luscious curves.

A jolt went through his body. He lowered his arms, resisting the urge to touch her. If his hand ended up in the wrong place, he'd be in serious danger of getting his face slapped.

With a little gasp, she drew back, thrusting a small cardboard box between them. "Matches," she said. "They were on the hearth. Muriel wanted me to bring them to you."

"Thanks." Forcing himself to be cool, he took the box and followed her back to the kitchen, where it was light enough to see a little. Shane's pulse was still racing. There in the dark hallway, she'd been so close, so tempting. What would've happened if he'd been crazy enough to pull her close and kiss her—Kylie Summerfield, the girl he'd wanted to kiss since he was Hunter's age? The one girl he'd never dared touch?

But what was he thinking? This wasn't the right time to get involved. It wasn't the right place or the right woman. Red lights all the way.

"Hold this." He handed her one of the longer candles. She kept it steady while he struck a match and lit the wick. The flame caught the wax and flickered upward, casting her face in a golden glow. She'd been a pretty girl in high school. Now, bathed in candlelight, she was stunning—and all woman.

"We need something to hold it up. There's a Mason jar by the sink. That should work." She hurried away from him and came back with the candle leaning against the inside rim of the jar.

"Hang on." Shane lit a second candle from the flame of the first. Sticking the end in a soda bottle Kylie had found, he carried it into the living room and set it on the hearth. As in many older homes, the opening of the fireplace had been filled with a cast-iron fireplace insert.

"Without the furnace going, we'll need some heat," he told Muriel. "Tell me where I can find some dry wood and I'll make us a fire."

"No need for so much work, Cowboy," Muriel said. "Henry always carries out the ashes and keeps the insert stoked with wood. All you'll need to do is open the front, check the damper, and light a match. If you need more wood, there's some in that box in the corner."

"Henry takes good care of this place," Kylie said. "You're lucky to have him."

"Oh, indeed I am. I don't know how I'd have managed without him all these years." Muriel pulled her hand-knitted afghan tighter around her shoulders. "I do hope he'll be warm enough out there in that trailer."

"Henry knows how to take care of himself. He'll be fine." Crouching in front of the hearth,

Shane opened the cast-iron door of the fireplace insert. It was as Muriel had said. The wood chunks were skillfully laid with newspaper and kindling underneath. After making sure the damper was open, all he had to do was light a match. Within minutes a crackling blaze was warming the room.

Shane made himself comfortable on the couch. Hunter wandered in with his phone and settled in a corner.

"Now this is cozy!" Kylie sipped the last of her lukewarm cocoa. "The old days must've been like this. Candles for light, a fireplace to keep warm . . ."

"And no TV to watch." Amy's voice reflected her sour mood.

"When I first came here as a little girl, we didn't have anything like TV, or even a radio," Muriel said. "The first summer, we lived in a tent while my father built the oldest part of this house, with the kitchen and bedroom, and a sleeping loft for me and my brother. Even after it was done, we didn't have electricity till the power company strung a line out here. That first winter we kept warm with the old iron stove my mother used for cooking. It had a tank on one side—a 'water jacket,' they called it. It heated water for dishes and our Saturday-night bath. I was about your age, Hunter, before we finally got an indoor bathroom."

That got Hunter's attention. "You mean you had to go outside to—"

"That's right. We had an outhouse—'privy' was the polite word for it—behind where the machine shed is now. On cold winter nights, it could seem like a very long walk. Sometimes when we went out there, we could hear coyotes howling. I remember how they used to scare me."

"Were you pioneers?" Amy asked.

"Pioneers?" Muriel chuckled. "I'm not quite as old as that. But it was after a time called the Great Depression when a lot of people were out of work. It was a common thing to be poor. My father got this piece of farmland from a man who had to move away. He traded our old truck for it. We were lucky to have land, but we were poor, too."

"I bet you at least had a Christmas tree," Amy said. "Everybody should have a Christmas tree, even if they're poor."

Kylie sighed. "I hear you, Amy. Believe me, I haven't given up."

"We didn't have money for a tree," Muriel said. "But there was usually a party with a tree and Christmas carols at the church. If we were lucky, we got a few pieces of candy and an orange. But we didn't get many presents. I remember one year the present I got was a pair of warm socks my mother had knitted. I do believe I still have those socks somewhere. They have a few holes now, but they kept my feet warm for a long time." There was a catch in her voice. "We didn't have much in those days, but we knew what we had was precious."

Muriel's hands kept busy as she talked. In the faint light, Shane could see a gray wool sock taking shape beneath her knitting needles.

"When my mother died, I was just fourteen and had to do the cooking and take care of the house," she said. "I managed to finish high school but couldn't go to college. When my brother— that would be your grandfather, Kylie—was seventeen, he took a job as a cowboy on one of the big ranches so we'd have a little money coming in. Even then there was never quite enough."

"Are you telling us kids that we don't have it so bad?" Amy stood, her hands clenched at her sides. "Not even if our dad died in the war and we had to leave our nice house in California and come to this cold, awful place where there's *nothing* to do? Last Christmas was bad. This Christmas is going to be worse! This is the worst time in my life!"

"That's enough, young lady!" Kylie was on her feet. "We're lucky to be here. You should be grateful to have a roof over your head and people who care about you. Go upstairs to your room and think about that for a while."

"My room will be freezing!"

"You've got plenty of blankets. You'll be warm enough in bed. If you leave the door open, you might even get a little heat from downstairs. Go on. We'll talk in the morning."

"It's dark on the stairs!"

"You'll get enough light from the kitchen to find your way. And the snow will reflect some light through the bedroom window. You'll be fine, Amy."

"It's not fair!" Amy flung back the words as she dashed upstairs.

In the silence that followed, Shane told himself he was well out of this drama. But then, in the firelight, he glimpsed Kylie's stricken face. She hadn't asked for any of this, he reminded himself. Fate had dealt her and her children a brutal blow. She was doing her best to help her family survive. It had to be tough.

In school he'd admired Kylie Summerfield for her beauty and intelligence. Now he'd discovered one more quality to admire—her courage. But that didn't mean he shouldn't keep his distance. Come spring, with luck, he'd have a buyer for the ranch and could start planning the rest of his life—the life of freedom and adventure he'd always dreamed of.

"I'm sorry, Aunt Muriel." Kylie fought back tears of frustration. "You've done so much for us. Amy should know better than to talk to you like that."

Muriel's knitting had fallen to her lap. She waved a hand in dismissal. "Don't worry about it, dear. She's young, she's been through a lot, and this old place isn't much like home. But she'll settle in. Just give her time."

"It's hard to see her hurting—but that's no excuse for hurting other people, especially you, when you've literally saved our lives." She glanced at her son, who was still texting. "That goes for you, too, Hunter. Tomorrow morning you're both getting a lesson in manners."

"Huh?" Hunter glanced up, then shrugged. "Whatever."

Muriel laid her knitting on the arm of the rocker and pushed herself to her feet. "Well, if you youngsters will excuse me, it's been a long day, and there's only so much I can get done in the dark. I'll see you in the morning."

"Will you be all right in the dark? I can walk you to your room," Shane offered.

"Thanks, Cowboy, but I've spent seventy-five years in this house and I know my way around. When I get old enough to need your help, I'll let you know." Carrying one of the candles, she tottered down the hallway toward her bedroom.

"Well, there's nothing to do down here except be bored," Hunter said. "I might as well go, too."

"Go on, then. Tomorrow will be better. You'll see."

"That's what you always say. And it's never

true, so you might as well stop lying about it." Hunter scuffed his way toward the stairs, dragging his feet.

Torn, Kylie gazed after him. She'd just sent both her children to bed angry tonight. After all they'd been through, how could she blame them for feeling the way they did?

She stood. "I hope you won't mind," she apologized to Shane. "I think I'd better go upstairs and do some peacemaking."

"Go ahead. If you decide to come back down, you'll find me right here by the fire."

Kylie picked up the Mason jar that held the candle and trudged up the stairs. Moving to Texas had been their only option after losing the house; and Muriel had been wonderfully welcoming. But how could she justify staying here when her children were so miserable?

What would she do if things didn't get better for them?

On the landing, the sound of blowing wind and snow pelting the roof was even louder. The candle flame cast dancing shadows on the wall as she moved down the hall. Hunter wouldn't be afraid, or at least he wouldn't show it. But Amy might be terrified.

The door to Amy's room stood open. Kylie stepped inside. Snowflakes spattered the panes of the single window. From the mound of blankets on the bed came the sound of muffled sobs.

"Amy?" She set the candle on the nightstand, sank onto the edge of the mattress and slowly pulled back the covers. Amy's face was buried in the pillow. "Are you okay, honey?"

Amy turned over, her face was wet, her eyes swollen. "Why do so many bad things have to happen to us? I didn't ask for Daddy to die. And I didn't ask to leave our house and come to this place. It's awful here. Aunt Muriel is nice, but Hunter and I don't have any friends or anyplace to go. We don't even have a Christmas tree or any presents to put under it." She sat up in bed, wiping her eyes with the sleeve of her pajama top. "When I try to be honest and tell you how I feel, all you do is get mad at me."

Kylie hugged the small, trembling body. "I'm sorry, sweetheart," she murmured. "And I wasn't mad because you were being honest. I was upset at you for hurting Aunt Muriel's feelings, after she's been so good to us."

"I know that now. I'm sorry." Amy started to cry again.

Kylie smoothed her daughter's damp, tangled hair. "I'd do anything to give you all the things you want, Amy. But for now, all we can do is hang on, make the best of things, and wait for better times. Things will get better, I promise. Someday you'll be a grown woman. You'll tell your children about this Christmas and the things you learned from it."

Amy sighed. "Maybe. But right now. I feel so bad my stomach hurts."

"You're not sick, are you?"

"No. Just sad."

"Well, go to sleep now." Kylie kissed her, eased her back onto the pillow and tucked the covers around her. "Tomorrow's another day."

"You always say that . . ." Amy's voice trailed off as she closed her eyes. Taking the candle, Kylie tiptoed into the hall and down to Hunter's room. She found her son fast asleep. Hunter's way of coping was to act as if he didn't care. But she knew he was hurting, too.

As the candle burned lower, she made her way back down the stairs to the living room. She'd done her best to keep her children close after their father's death, and to give them a good life. But tonight she felt like a failure. Somehow she had to find a way to lighten their crushed spirits.

Exhausted, Kylie sank onto the sofa. Even keeping her eyes open took more strength than she had left. Outside, the storm was unrelenting, battering the house as if to tear it apart.

"Are you all right?" Shane's voice startled her. After the stress of dealing with her children, she'd almost forgotten he was there, sitting at the other end of the sofa with his arm along the back.

"I will be as soon as I take a few breaths. I love

my children, but trying to make them happy can be like banging my head against a wall."

"Maybe you're trying too hard."

"Listen to you, Shane Taggart." She opened her eyes and turned on the couch to face him. "As I remember, you were an only child growing up, and you told me today that you never had children of your own. So what makes you a child-raising expert?"

The firelight glowed bronze on the planes of his sculpted face. "I may not be an expert, Kylie, but I've got eyes and ears. Your kids have been through a rough time, losing their dad and their home. They have every reason to be unhappy. Maybe you should just step back and let them work through it."

"Fat lot you know." Leaning forward, Kylie watched the crimson glow of the fire through the iron insert's mica panes.

"I may not know much," he said, "but I know what I see—a beautiful woman beating herself up because she can't protect her children from the bad things that happen in life—a woman taking care of everybody but herself."

"So now you're Sigmund Freud—or is it Dr. Phil? You don't know me, Shane. You don't know anything about me." Kylie meant to sound defiant, but she could feel herself crumbling inside. The man was getting to her.

"Not true. I've known you since you were five

years old. For little Kylie Summerfield, anything short of an A-plus was a failure. Something tells me you haven't changed that much."

"Well, I wouldn't give myself an A-plus for today. I burned a batch of cookies, couldn't find a Christmas tree, wrecked your precious bike, and came close to having meltdowns with both my children."

He shook his head. "I'm surprised you're not blaming yourself for the storm and the power outage. Take it easy on yourself, Kylie. You can't hit a home run every time."

"But don't you see? I can't give up. I have to keep trying. And now it's almost . . . Christmas." Her voice broke. She was trembling, on the verge of tears.

"Come here, lady." His arm, which had rested along the back of the couch, reached down to circle her shoulder and pull her toward him. "You need a buddy hug. Don't worry, I'm not out to take advantage of you. Just relax. Let it go."

If she resisted, it was only for an instant. The solid warmth of his arm around her shoulders felt like something she needed. His subtle scent, a blend of snow and motor oil and fresh hay, stirred memories of the old days, growing up happy and secure in Branding Iron. She remembered the Christmas holidays, the stockings by the fire-place, the glittering tree, and the excitement of opening her gifts.

His hand moved to the back of her neck. Strong fingers massaged the aching muscles. A little purring sound rose in her throat. "That feels wonderful. Where did you learn to do that?"

"I learned massage to help my father after his stroke," he said. "You're all knotted up. Just close your eyes and breathe."

Kylie exhaled, feeling the tension drain out of her shoulders. "I'm really, really sorry I wrecked your bike," she said.

The sound of blowing snow filled the brief silence. "Accidents happen. If it can be fixed, I'll fix it. If not . . ." His voice trailed off. He paused as if weighing what he was about to say next. "When we were in high school, I thought about asking you out. I wanted to, but I knew I wasn't the kind of boy you'd want to be seen with. I couldn't handle being turned down by Little Miss Perfect."

Jolted by his revelation, Kylie pressed her lips together to keep from confessing her own secret crush. If she were to tell Shane the truth, he might take it as an invitation—and she wasn't ready for that. She twisted the simple gold band on her finger—the wedding ring she'd worn for the past fourteen years. His eyes took in the gesture. His hand returned to the back of the couch.

"I take it you haven't started dating again," he said.

Kylie shook her head. "I've got better things to

do than beat the bushes for single men. And even if I did meet someone, how could I do that to my children? They're already dealing with so much. A new man, or men, in their lives—it wouldn't be right."

"Hearing that doesn't surprise me. And knowing you wouldn't have settled for less, I imagine your husband was a fine man."

"He was." Kylie's throat tightened, as it did whenever she spoke about Brad. "But we had to share him with the army. He spent more time away than he did with his family. While he was gone, I had to manage on my own—not so different from now, except that now we know he's not coming back. He's buried in Arlington National Cemetery—that was what he always wanted." She gazed down at her hands in the firelight, wondering if she'd revealed too much. "But that's enough about me. Tell me what you've been doing all these years."

He stretched his long legs, resting his stocking-clad feet on the raised brick hearth. One wool sock had a dime-sized hole in the toe. "Not much to tell. My plan after graduation was to head for the Gulf Coast and work for a while, maybe on an oil rig or a shrimp trawler, till I could save enough money to travel. I was packing up to leave when my dad had a stroke. It turned out to be bad. There was no way I could leave him, especially since my mother had passed away years before. Now that he's gone, too . . ." Shane shook his head. "It seems like all I've ever done in my life is run that ranch. If I don't cut loose now, I never will."

"Is that why you never got married? I remember how the girls used to chase you. You must've had plenty of offers."

"Maybe. But only from the desperate ones. Face it, chasing a boy is one thing. Choosing a life partner is something else. And I'm not what you'd call great husband material, am I?"

"No comment."

He laughed. Not just a chuckle, but a deep, masculine belly laugh that Kylie could feel where she sat next to him. "Now that's what I call honesty! I always did like that about you. You never tried to butter me up like other girls did by saying things you didn't mean."

"Maybe I should've tried harder," she said. "Maybe if I had, you'd have taken me for a ride on your motorcycle. Maybe you'd have taken me down by the riverbank with a six-pack of beer, like you did those other girls."

He stopped laughing.

Heaven help her, what did she just say?

"I wouldn't have taken you down by the riverbank, Kylie. You were too good for that. If I'd taken you for a ride, it would have been down the middle of Main Street, so the whole town could see the classy girl that worthless bum Shane Taggart had on the back of his bike."

Something tightened in Kylie's chest, quickening her pulse. His face was dangerously close—so close that she felt an aching urge to tempt fate. Her eyes closed. Her chin tilted toward him. She was dimly conscious of the storm swirling outside.

Her heart thundered as she felt his warm breath and the first nibbling brush of his lips on hers. His hands didn't move to pull her close. Only their mouths touched. She tasted cocoa and marshmallow foam as he kissed her with a gentle hunger that awakened a deep throbbing need.

Her conscience shrilled that this was wrong for so many reasons—her children, upstairs in their rooms, the ring on her finger, the grave in Arlington, and the wrecked motorcycle outside in the shed. But right now, all she could think of was wanting more.

She leaned into his kiss, responding in spite of herself. For an instant, his breath caught. He stiffened, then eased her away from him. His dark eyes burned in the firelight.

"This isn't helping either of us, Kylie. If you know me, and if you know what's good for you, you'll get up this minute, climb those stairs to your room, and stay there till daylight."

She drew back, her cheeks blazing. "Shane, I didn't mean to—"

"Neither did I." His throat moved as he swallowed. "I'll see you tomorrow. Go."

"This never happened!" She flung the words back at him as she fled, stumbling up the stairs to her room, feeling her way in the dark.

Chapter Five

December 23

Gray light, filtering through Muriel's lace curtains, woke Shane to a leaden dawn. The room was cold, the house quiet, with no sign that the power had come back on.

After spending most of the night trying to get comfortable on the too-short couch, he ached in every muscle. It was a relief for him to fling off the quilt, stand up, and stretch his legs. The stillness outside told him the storm had passed. His truck would be buried in snow. He would dig it out, of course, but if the drifts were too deep on the road, driving it anywhere could be another story.

Meanwhile, there'd be paths to shovel and the generator to get working. Henry was going to need his help. But the first order of the day would be to get some heat into the house for the women and kids.

The fire had gone cold, but he found some logs, along with kindling and newspaper, in the bucket next to the hearth. Shane gave silent thanks to Henry's foresight as he laid a new fire and lit it with a match. The old man really did take good care of Muriel and her property.

With the fire going, Shane wandered into the kitchen to find his coat and boots. The well-worn cowboy boots, which weren't made for snow, were still damp, but they'd have to do. At least the socks on his feet were dry, and the sheepskin coat would be warm.

Slipping his boots and coat on, he glanced around the kitchen. No power would mean no hot water for coffee. Too bad. But never mind, he wanted to be gone from the house when Kylie came downstairs. After last night, facing her would be awkward.

He couldn't say he regretted kissing her—she'd clearly needed kissing, and her lips had been as delicious as ripe strawberries. But he had a rule against kissing any woman who wore a wedding ring—even a widow. And last night he'd broken it. Kylie might be legally free. But that band of gold around her finger was a clear signal that her heart belonged to another man.

Pulling his leather work gloves out of his coat pockets, he opened the back door and stepped out onto the porch. The sky was clearing, but the cold was bitter enough to sting his skin, and the snow was more than two feet deep. He couldn't remember a time when this part of Texas had seen so much. Around his truck, which he'd abandoned in the middle of the yard, it was over the hubcaps, with more snow piled high on the hood, the cab, and the bed. Time to find a shovel and start digging.

Slogging through knee-deep snow, he made it to the machine shed, where he found Henry tinkering with the gasoline-powered generator. The old man glanced back at him with a grin. "Almost got it," he said. "I'm hoping an oil change and a fresh starter battery will do the trick."

"Holler if you need any help," Shane said. "I'll be busy shoveling."

"Knock yourself out. Shovel's hanging on that far wall."

Shane started with a path from the shed to Henry's trailer, and from there back to the house. He was almost to the back porch when he saw the back porch light flicker on. The generator was working. It wouldn't be like having full power. They could only use electricity for essentials, but it was better than nothing. Maybe by nightfall, the power company would make it out here to fix the problem—if they could get through the drifting snow.

After he'd shoveled a path around the house and down the front walk to the mailbox, he started clearing the snow off his pickup. The storm had been a wet one—good for the land, but heavy to shovel. Shane was used to hard work, but he could tell he'd be hurting later on. Taking a breather, he paused to survey the snow-buried road out front. Even if he could shovel a path out of the yard, he'd be lucky to make it a hundred yards without getting stuck. Muriel hadn't owned a horse in years, and Shane doubted he could survive the five-mile distance to his ranch slogging through deep snow in wet cowboy boots. Since the town of Branding Iron had no snowplow, it was anybody's guess when the road would be cleared.

He'd left extra food and water for his animals, but he hadn't planned on being gone longer than overnight. He needed some way to get back and take care of them.

"How about some hot breakfast?" Kylie had come out onto the porch. Wrapped in a blue fleece jacket, with tousled hair and no makeup, she looked fresh and pretty. The memory of last night slammed Shane like a gut punch. *Forget it,* he told himself. *Like the lady said, it never happened.*

"Breakfast? That sounds just dandy!" Henry had come out of the shed. Trudging along the path Shane had shoveled, he reached the porch, where the two men stomped the snow off their boots.

Shane followed Kylie into the warm kitchen, inhaling the aromas of bacon and fresh coffee. Kylie turned away from him, avoiding eye contact while she tended the bacon and scrambled the eggs. Muriel was buttering toast at the counter. Amy and Hunter sat at the table; they looked even gloomier than they had the night before.

"So, what's with you two?" Shane poured coffee for himself and Henry and set the cups on the table, then pulled out a chair and sat down. "You look like you just missed the last flight to Disney World."

His attempt at humor fell flat. The children glanced at each other and rolled their eyes. "We can't go out in the snow," Hunter said. "Mom ordered winter coats and gloves and boots for us online. She had them sent here so we wouldn't have to take them in the move. They haven't come. Neither have our Christmas presents."

Kylie glanced around. Only now did Shane notice the strain that tightened her lovely mouth and etched shadows beneath her eyes. "I checked the Internet on my phone this morning. The shipper guaranteed to have the packages here before Christmas, but evidently the storm's covered most of the Midwest. There's a notice up that everything's been delayed."

Amy's big blue eyes, a match to her mother's, brimmed with tears. "It's not fair!" she stormed.

"This is going to be the worst Christmas ever!"

Kylie looked stricken. "It's my fault. If I'd ordered everything sooner, the packages would have arrived days ago."

"Don't blame yourself, dear." Muriel patted her arm. "You were dealing with the move, doing the best you could. And you certainly didn't cause the storm. Sooner or later, the packages will arrive, and when they do, it'll be like having a second Christmas."

"That doesn't help us much, right now," Hunter said. "I've never seen so much snow. And I can't even go outside to make a snowball."

"I've got an idea, Hunter." Muriel put the plate of buttered toast on the table. "You're a big boy for your age, and my father was small for a man. I put his winter clothes and boots in the attic. Maybe some of his things will fit you."

Hunter hesitated. His sister wrinkled her nose. "Gross! That would be creepy, wearing some dead person's clothes!"

"Amy, that's enough," Kylie said. "You know, that doesn't sound like a bad idea, Hunter. Those old clothes might not be the latest style, but at least they'd be warm—unless you'd rather stay in the house."

Hunter reached for a slice of toast. "Okay. I'll take a look after breakfast. At least maybe I'll get to go outside."

Kylie set the bacon and scrambled eggs on the

table. "Fine, and as long as you're out there, you can take your turn at shoveling snow."

"What about me?" Amy demanded. "I want to go outside, too."

Kylie and Muriel exchanged glances and shook their heads. Shane guessed that nothing in the house would come close to fitting Amy's small frame.

"We'll find something fun to do inside," Kylie said. "How would you like to help me make some Christmas cookies?"

Amy sighed, saying nothing. She and Hunter weren't bad kids, Shane reflected as he downed his bacon and eggs. They'd had their young lives cruelly uprooted and were doing an honest job of expressing how they felt about it. It was Kylie, holding it all in and trying to make everything fine, who made him worry.

But this was no time to get involved—especially with a curvy blond bundle of spunk whose lips tasted like springtime, and whose kiss had made him ache for more. She was wearing a ring, and he already had enough problems of his own.

"What will you need my help with this morning, Henry?" he asked.

"Nothing that can't wait." The old man poured more coffee. "You might as well go tend your own place—or at least try to get there."

"I figured you'd say that," Shane said. "I don't

know if my truck can make it through the snow, but I've got to try. Can I borrow a shovel to use in case I get stuck?"

"Sure," Henry said. "But hold on, I just remembered something that might work better. Come out to the shed when you've had your fill and I'll show it to you."

By the time the men finished eating, Hunter had gone to check the clothes in the attic, and Amy had been sent upstairs to make her bed and straighten her room. Kylie had shooed Muriel out of the kitchen and was busy cleaning up. Shane's eyes followed the sure movements of her small, neat hands and admired the sway of her hips as she carried the dishes to the sink. *Bad idea,* he scolded himself. There was no denying he was intrigued. But she'd barely met his gaze or spoken more than a couple of words to him this morning. The message was clear. If he was looking for signals, she wasn't sending any.

Shane followed Henry along the shoveled path to the machine shed. He averted his eyes from his smashed motorcycle, which was propped against one wall. He would have to deal with the bike later. For now, he had more urgent concerns.

Henry led him to the back corner of the shed, where a canvas tarp covered a bulky object. "Almost forgot I had this," he said. "Fellow who came down from Wyoming gave it to me in trade for some work, when he couldn't pay. I never figured I'd have any use for the blasted thing—till now."

He pulled off the tarp. Shane swore in surprise. "I'll be damned! It's a snowmobile! Does it work?"

"The man said it did, but I never tried it out. No reason to till today. But I checked to make sure the fluids were drained. What d'you say we fill 'er up and try 'er out?"

Shane helped the old man put gas, oil, and antifreeze in the tanks. The vehicle, with skis in front and a set of tracks in back, would be a great solution to getting around in the snow—if they could get it working.

Together they pushed the machine outside, clear of the shed. The key was in the ignition. When Henry tried it, the engine sputtered, then caught with a roar that startled a cloud of blackbirds out of a nearby cottonwood.

Conversation was impossible with the engine running. Henry switched it off. "So far, so good. Ever drive one of these things?"

"No, but it can't be much different from a motorcycle. Let me try it." Shane climbed aboard. By the time he'd started it up and made two circles in the yard, he was already feeling comfortable with the machine. Stopping by the shed, he turned off the engine. "Not bad," he said. "You're a lifesaver, Henry. Guess I'll be heading back to my ranch for a bit. Give my thanks to Muriel."

"Wow!" Hunter had come out onto the back porch. Dressed in an old plaid mackinaw, wool mittens, rubber boots, and a cap that covered his ears and tied under the chin, he looked like a relic from the 1940s, but at least he was warm. "That looks like fun!"

"Fun, but cold," Shane said. "Behave yourself and maybe I'll give you a ride on it later."

"How about now?" The boy paused, as if remembering his manners. "Please."

"Later, maybe. I was about to run over to my ranch and do the chores."

"I could come with you and help. With all the snow, you'll need an extra pair of hands." He looked so desperately eager that Shane's heart began to soften. The boy needed something to do besides text and play games on his phone. And Kylie needed a break from mothering her bored, discontented teenage son.

"Ask your mother," he said. "If it's okay with her . . ."

Before he could finish the sentence, Hunter had already disappeared into the house. Moments later he was back, his face lit by a happy grin. "She said yes! Let's go!"

"Fine. Hop on behind me." Shane was used to supervising the high-school boys who worked summers on his ranch haying and tending cattle.

Kylie's son wouldn't be much different, he told himself. Just a little younger.

The snowmobile had a seat for a passenger behind the driver. Shane waited while Hunter climbed into place. "Hold on tight. Here we go." The engine roared to life again. Shane put the vehicle in gear and opened the throttle. With snow flying around them, and Hunter whooping like an old-time Apache on the warpath, they shot down the drive and swung down the road toward the Taggart ranch.

"It isn't fair!" Amy scowled out the kitchen window as the snowmobile roared down the road and vanished from sight.

Kylie sighed as she gathered the ingredients for sugar cookies. The worst thing about hearing Amy's words, again and again, was that they were so often true.

"I know, sweetheart," she said. "Right now, life doesn't seem fair. But things will get better, you'll see."

"But why does Hunter get to have all the fun? He gets to go on the snowmobile and I have to stay cooped up in the house like a prisoner."

Why? Because he's older. Because your mother wasn't smart enough to order your winter clothes earlier. And because, for the first time since your father died, Hunter looked so happy that I couldn't say no.

None of those answers would satisfy her daughter, Kylie knew.

"You'll get your turn at something fun, I promise, Amy," she said. "For now, how about helping me make some Christmas cookies?"

"Maybe we won't even burn them." Amy turned away from the window, her sour expression saying more than words.

"We won't burn these cookies." Kylie was determined to stay cheerful. "I've asked Aunt Muriel to work her magic with the stove. While they're baking, we'll be right here keeping an eye on them."

"Since that oven door doesn't have a window, we're going to need X-ray vision," Amy said. "Maybe that's what Aunt Muriel's got."

"Did I hear my name mentioned?" Muriel tottered into the kitchen with her knitting bag and took a seat at the table.

"I was about to preheat the oven," Kylie said. "The cookie recipe says three hundred seventy-five degrees. That's the temperature I set yesterday when the cookies burned. So tell me what to do."

"Set it for three forty-five," Muriel said. "And it's best if you don't open the oven till the cookies are done."

Kylie blinked at her. "But how can you tell they're done if you don't open the oven?"

"Why, by the smell, of course! How else?"

Muriel opened her bag and took out the sock she was knitting. Her needles clicked in the stillness of the kitchen as Kylie set the stove and began to cream the butter and sugar. Amy glanced at the recipe and began measuring the dry ingredients into a smaller bowl.

"So, what do you think of the cowboy?" Muriel asked. "He's really something, isn't he?"

Kylie's breath caught for an instant. She felt heat flood her face, remembering last night's kiss and her fevered response. "He's okay, I guess. I might be more enthused about him if I hadn't wrecked his motorcycle."

"Oh, he'll get over that," Muriel said. "I can tell he likes you."

"That's silly." Kylie kept her back toward the table to hide her blazing cheeks. "He hardly pays any attention to me."

"That's how I know he likes you," Muriel said. "He's playing it cool."

Amy giggled.

"You're imagining things, Aunt Muriel." Kylie broke two eggs into the bowl. Her hands were a trifle unsteady. Good grief, was the old darling matchmaking? "I had mixed feelings about letting Hunter go with him today. Remembering what Shane was like in high school, I can't believe he'd be a good influence on a growing boy."

"What was he like?" Amy was becoming interested.

"He was the town bad boy, always breaking rules and getting in trouble. I still remember when he showed up after Christmas break with a tattoo of an eagle on his shoulder. I don't know where he got it, but he was eighteen by then so he didn't need permission."

"A tattoo? Wow!" Amy grinned.

"It almost got him expelled. The principal made him keep it covered, even in gym class. He had to wear a T-shirt with sleeves."

"Has he still got the tattoo?" Amy asked.

"How on earth would I know?" Kylie's color deepened.

"Oh, I've seen it," Muriel said. "He takes his shirt off to haul hay in the summer. Oh, my . . ." Her needles slowed, then resumed their regular clicking rhythm. "Anyway, I can't imagine his being a bad influence on Hunter. The cowboy's outgrown those wild old days. Last year the city council even asked him to run for sheriff. He turned them down, probably because he'd have been running against his friend, Ben Marsden. But it says a lot that they'd even ask. And he does so much for Henry and me. He comes by to check on us almost every day."

The woman was definitely matchmaking. Kylie didn't want to hurt Muriel's feelings, but she wasn't ready for another man in her life, especially a free spirit like Shane Taggart. As for Shane, saddling him with a wife and stepchildren would be like harnessing a wild stallion to a plow.

True, last night's kiss had shot hot tingles all the way to her toes. But a lasting relationship demanded a lot more than kisses—more than either of them was prepared to give.

"Ben Marsden." Kylie deliberately changed the subject. "I remember him from school. All state in football. He won a college scholarship, wanted to play in the NFL. What brought him back to Branding Iron?"

"Bad luck," Muriel said. "He blew out his knee his junior year in college. Henry was watching the game when it happened. I remember him saying, 'That boy's done for good.' And he was. He married a beautiful girl, but that didn't work out, either. Now she's in Austin, and he's back in Branding Iron with joint custody of their little boy."

"What a sad story," Kylie said. "Everybody in our class thought Ben would be the one to set the world on fire."

"Well, he might not have managed to do that," Muriel said. "But he's a darned good sheriff."

"I still can't believe he and Shane are friends now. They couldn't stand each other in school. I still remember the day they got in a big fist-fight—now I can't even remember what it was about. Probably a girl."

"A fight?" Amy was wide-eyed. "What happened?"

"Not much. They both wound up in the principal's office, Shane with a black eye and Ben with a bloody nose. How did they get past that time?"

Muriel shrugged and smiled. "People grow up," she said.

With the cookie dough mixed, Kylie rolled it out on a floured board and let Amy use the cookie cutters to stamp out stars, bells, snowmen, and reindeer shapes. When the two cookie sheets were full, she slid them, with a silent prayer, into the oven and closed the door. Something, even if it was only cookies, just had to turn out all right today.

Shane swung the snowmobile into the yard, pulled up behind the house, and switched off the engine. The five-mile ride from Muriel's place to his ranch had been downright fun, with snow spraying around them and Hunter whooping and hollering all the way.

The yard was an expanse of dazzling white, marred only by bird tracks etched across its surface. Everything looked peaceful, but Shane was anxious to check on his animals. "All right, fun's over," he said to Hunter. "Now it's time to work."

The boy climbed off the snowmobile, giving Shane room to swing a leg over and step to the ground. Shane blessed Henry for the loan of the vehicle. The machine would make it possible to take care of his ranch and still work on the bike at Muriel's. While the snow lasted, it might also be fun to take Kylie's kids for rides on it. If some warm clothes could be found, Amy would certainly demand her turn.

But where had that idea come from? If he valued his freedom, getting mixed up with Kylie and her needy little brood would be the craziest thing he could do.

There were plenty of other women out there, he reminded himself—women with no children and no expectations beyond having a little fun. But his instincts told him Kylie was a woman who played for keeps—and he'd never been a "for keeps" kind of man.

The snow was well over their knees. Shane's soaked feet had gone numb, but at least he had some winter boots and dry socks in the house.

"What do you want me to do?" Hunter asked. He was coated with snow and his teeth were chattering, but the boy wasn't complaining or asking to go in the house and get warm. His father, as a military man, had probably stressed discipline in his son. Not a bad thing as long as it wasn't overdone.

Shane began breaking a trail toward the back steps. "There should be a couple of shovels on the porch. While I'm changing my boots, you can start shoveling a path from the house to the barn."

"Sure. And thanks for letting me come with you, Shane. Is it okay if I call you that?"

"It's fine. Everybody else does. But you might not be feeling so thankful by the time we finish the path." Shane passed the boy one of the shovels he kept on the screened back porch. "Get started. I'll be out to help you in a couple of minutes."

"Okay. Where do you want the path?"

"You look like a smart boy. That's up to you."

Shane stomped the snow off his boots, unlocked the back door and walked into the house. The place was cold—not much he could do about that until the power that ran the furnace came on. He couldn't check e-mail on his computer, either. Too bad he didn't have one of those newfangled cell phones that had Internet access. It might be a good idea to get one before he left on his road trip.

In the kitchen and bathroom he turned on the faucets to a trickle to keep the water moving in the cold pipes. A glance out the kitchen window assured him that Hunter was shoveling snow like a trooper. As soon as he could get something dry on his feet, he'd go back out and join the boy.

In his bedroom, he pulled his oiled work boots out of the closet and found a pair of thick wool socks in the dresser drawer. Sitting on the edge of the bed, he pried off his cowboy boots, peeled his wet socks off his chilled feet and put on the dry ones. He was just tightening the laces on his work boots when the landline phone on his nightstand rang. He reached for it. At least something in the house worked.

"Hello?" Maybe it was somebody calling from Muriel's place.

"Hi, Shane." The female voice was low, sexy and vaguely familiar. "Long time, no see."

"Uh, hi." Shane racked his brain, trying to place the voice.

"Silly! It's me, Holly! I'm in town visiting my folks for the week, and when I saw you were still in the phone book . . ."

"Oh, sure. Great to hear from you." How could he forget Holly Murchison, one of the prettiest— and wildest—girls he'd ever dated. The last time she'd been in town, a couple of years ago, they'd caught up on old times, in more ways than one. But he'd barely thought of her since. "Still working in the governor's office?" he asked her.

"For now. But I'm moving up in the world. Going to Washington, DC, for a job interview next month. It's just secretarial work, but in the right place, anything can happen."

Yes, anything, Shane thought. Like hooking up with some wealthy, powerful Washington guy. He'd enjoyed Holly, but he knew he was only a pit stop on her fast-track to fame and fortune.

"Just wondering if you were busy tonight,"

she said. "We could get together for drinks, or . . . whatever. Her implication was clear. But for some reason, the idea of a one-night stand didn't hold much appeal.

"Sorry, Holly, but I'm dealing with a lot right now," he said. "The power's off out here, and, with the snow, I need to make sure my animals are all right, as well as checking on my neighbors. Their boy is outside right now, shoveling a path to the barn. I need to get out there and help him."

"I see."

Shane could hear the hiss of her breath as she reined in her temper. A woman as gorgeous as Holly wasn't accustomed to being turned down. Maybe he should steer her toward Ben. But something told him Branding Iron's sheriff didn't need any more woman troubles.

"Well." Her voice was acid-tinged. "I guess I can always watch *Downton Abbey* reruns with my mother. Call me if you get lonesome and change your mind. You've got my number." The connec-tion went silent as the call ended.

He hung up the phone, finished tying his boots, and walked out onto the back porch. Hunter straightened as Shane came outside. He'd made fair progress shoveling but he looked cold and tired.

"Hey," Shane said, grabbing the spare shovel. "Let me give you a hand with that."

Muriel sniffed the cookie-scented air, paused, then sniffed again. "I do believe those cookies are done," she said. "Hurry, take them out before they get too brown."

Kylie switched off the stove, grabbed the oven mitt and a thick dish towel, and opened the oven door. The cookies looked perfect. Mindful of the hole in the mitt, she lifted the cookie sheets out of the oven and onto the counter.

"They look awesome!" Amy said. "When can we start decorating them?"

Kylie breathed a silent prayer of thanks. For the first time since leaving San Diego, Amy seemed excited about something. "They'll need to cool first. And we'll need to make some icing. I'll put a cube of butter out to soften. Have you got some powdered sugar, Aunt Muriel?"

"I believe so. There should be a bag of it in the bin, where you found the flour and sugar. But put a few plain cookies on a pie tin for Henry, would you? He doesn't like them too sweet."

Kylie used a spatula to lift four cookies onto a plate for Henry. Then she took a square of butter out of the fridge. Too bad she hadn't thought to buy those little tubs of premixed, colored icing at Shop Mart. They made decorating so much easier.

"While the cookies are cooling, dear, could I ask a favor? On a cold day like this, Henry would so enjoy warm cookies. Could you run that plate out to him? Now that the path is shoveled, you shouldn't need boots."

"I'd be happy to." Kylie covered the plate with foil, slipped on her fleece jacket, and went out the back door. By now, the sky had cleared to a bright, wintry blue. Snow sparkled diamond white in the sun. But the air turned her breath to puffs of white.

She hurried down the path to Henry's trailer and knocked on the door. No one answered. But now, as she listened, she could hear faint sounds of clattering metal coming from the machine shed. She raced back along the path to the shed. The sliding door was ajar. She pushed it open far enough to let her step inside; then she closed it behind her.

Henry was seated on a low stool, inspecting Shane's wrecked motorcycle by the light that fell through the windows. Kylie stood watching for a moment as he shifted the bent, broken parts, frowning thoughtfully.

"I'm so sorry for what happened," she said, breaking the silence. "Do you think it can be fixed?"

He turned his head, his startled look warming to a smile. "Don't know yet. But I do know how Shane loves this old bike. I'll do my best."

"He said if anybody could fix it, you could. Here, I brought you some warm cookies." She passed him the plate. "Muriel said you liked them without icing."

"Muriel always remembers." His blue eyes lit. He helped himself to a cookie and held the plate out to offer her one. Kylie shook her head. "Thanks, but these are all for you."

"Then I'll enjoy them while they're fresh out of the oven," he said. "If you don't mind keeping an old man company for a few minutes, you can take the plate back when you go. There's a chair behind you."

Kylie pulled the old kitchen chair closer and sat down. She'd been aware of Henry's presence for almost as long as she'd known Muriel. But he'd always been a little distant, a little shy; plus, he'd always seemed to be working. She'd never had the chance to sit and talk with him.

The machine shed was Henry's domain. Kylie glanced around at the racks of tools and parts, the ongoing projects. Everything was neat and orderly, with the touch of a man who took pride in his work.

"You've been part of the farm for as long as I can remember, Henry," she said, making conversation. "What brought you here in the first place?"

Henry munched down another cookie, his face a portrait of pleasure. "My family was from Branding Iron," he said. "But because there weren't many jobs for a young man, I joined the navy. I spent four years in the service, mostly as a machinist's mate. By the time I came home, my family was all gone, either dead or moved away. Muriel's dad needed a ranch hand and he offered me a place to live, so here I am."

"But Shane says you're the best mechanic he's ever known. You could've made more money working somewhere else, had a home, a family."

"This is my home. And Muriel's my family now. She needs me to look after the place and make sure she's safe. How could I go away and leave her to manage on her own?" He fell silent, a faraway look in his eyes.

Kylie gazed at the old man, pondering what she'd heard, sifting his words like a handful of newly discovered diamonds. Though it had been unspoken, she knew the truth—knew it beyond question.

Henry loved Muriel. He'd probably loved her for years, perhaps all his life. That was why he'd stayed. But he was a quiet man who kept his emotions private—a proud man, afraid, perhaps, of being rejected and sent away.

Even after all these years, there was no reason to believe he'd ever told her.

Chapter Six

By the time the shoveled path neared the barn, Shane's back muscles were burning. "You're holding up better than I am," he told Hunter. "Right now, I wouldn't mind being thirteen again."

"You wouldn't like it." Hunter scooped another shovelful of snow. "Being thirteen sucks, especially now. At least in California, I had friends. Here there's nobody to hang out with and nothing to do. I hate it."

"You'll make friends here," Shane said. "Once school starts in January, you'll be fine."

"But I'll be the new kid. Everybody picks on the new kid."

"True." Shane dug his shovel into the wet, heavy snow and hefted it upward. "You're liable to be tested at first. But if they tease you, don't be a victim. Make a joke of it or walk away. They'll soon get tired of it. If you show them who you really are, the best of them will want to be your friends, and the others won't matter."

Shane studied the boy's face as he pondered the well-meant advice. Hunter was right about one thing. Even under good conditions, being thirteen sucked. Kids could be cruel to any newcomer, especially one who might not fit in with the locals.

"What were things like for you when you were my age?" Hunter tossed another shovelful of snow.

Shane weighed his answer, knowing he couldn't tell the whole truth. When he was thirteen, his mother had been diagnosed with cancer. In the three years that followed, his parents' lives had revolved around her unsuccessful treatment, leaving young Shane to his own devices. The first time he'd been arrested—shoplifting a beer from a convenience store—he'd discovered that the bad-boy label lent him a certain cachet. The locker-room bullies left him alone, and the girls, especially the older, wilder ones, gave him looks that couldn't be misread. He'd always been big for his age, and the hormone express had come steaming in early. He'd lost his virginity at fifteen to a senior cheerleader and never looked back. None of that story was fit to tell Kylie's son. But lying, especially to kids, had never been his style.

"Things weren't great," he said. "I tried to play the tough guy, made a lot of mistakes and learned a lot of lessons the hard way. I hope you'll be smarter than I was and listen to your mother's advice. She's a sharp lady and wants the best for you. You're lucky to have her."

"Did you really know her in school?" Hunter asked.

"You bet. All the way from kindergarten through our senior year. She was the smartest, nicest, prettiest girl in our class. A loser like me wasn't fit to carry her books."

"And did you want to? Carry her books, I mean."

"All the boys did. But she was choosy, and she didn't choose me. Can't say I blamed her for that."

The conversation was getting a little too close to home. Shane was relieved to find that they'd reached the barn. He unlocked the sliding door. "Stay behind me," he said. "I need to make sure nothing's gotten loose in here."

Sunlight fell through the high windows below the roof. As Shane slid the door open, a horse nickered in its stall. Sheila jumped out of her box with a happy bark and came bounding to meet him.

"Hey, old girl, did you miss me? How's the family?" Shane reached down and scratched behind her silky ears.

"Wow! What a cool dog!" Hunter had come in behind him. "Look at those spots! Can I pet her?"

"Sure. She loves attention."

Hunter knelt in the straw, held out his hand, and made little coaxing sounds. Sheila went right to him. "I've never seen a dog like this," he said. "What kind is she?"

"Blue heeler. It's an Australian breed. Best cattle dogs on the planet."

Hunter patted Sheila, laughing when she rewarded him with wags and kisses. "Hey, look! She likes me!"

"I can tell," Shane said, chuckling. "So you like dogs, do you?"

"I love dogs. But we couldn't have one when Dad was in the army because we traveled a lot. We couldn't always take a dog with us. Amy likes dogs, too. Maybe Mom and Aunt Muriel will let us have one here."

"Could be. Wouldn't hurt to ask."

"Oh, wow!" Jumping up, Hunter raced toward the stalls. "You've got horses, too! Can I touch them?"

"Go ahead. Just don't move too fast. Horses don't like to be startled. The first one's a girl. Her name's Daisy."

Hunter reached over the gate of the first stall and stroked a finger down the face of Shane's bay mare. "I've never touched a horse before. Her nose is so soft. It's like—"

He jerked his hand away as the mare sneezed. "Oh, yuck!" He wiped his sprayed hand on his trousers.

Shane laughed. "If I'm still around come spring, I'll teach you and your sister how to ride them. Every Texas kid should learn to ride."

"Are you saying you might not be here?" The boy sounded stricken.

"I'm putting the ranch up for sale. Once it's

sold, I'll be off to see the country, like I've always wanted."

"Oh." Hunter kicked at the straw, his eyes downcast.

"For now, there's something else here you'll like," Shane said. "Come here. I'll show you Sheila's family." He motioned Hunter into the stall where he kept the puppy box. "Go on in and look," he said.

Hunter peered over the side of the box. "Oh, my gosh!" he gasped as the puppies came tumbling toward him. "Can I hold them?"

"Sure. They're old enough to go to their new homes."

Hunter picked up one of the little females, giggling as she wriggled and licked his face. "What would I have to do to earn one of these?"

"Sorry," Shane said. "The three girls are already spoken for. And this little rascal"—he scooped up the little male with one hand—"he's going to be my traveling partner. His name's Mickey."

Hunter reached out to take the male pup. Mickey licked the boy's chin and snuggled into his arms. "So you're keeping him," Hunter said.

"That's the plan."

"Too bad. He's the one I like the best. Is the mother going to have any more?"

"This'll be her last litter. Sorry you missed out. But these purebred cattle dogs are worth a lot of money. When you're ready to get a pup, you'll find plenty of good ones in shelters."

Hunter hung on to Mickey a little longer, then released him back into the box. "Now what?" he asked.

Shane raised an eyebrow. "You said you wanted to help with chores. When you keep animals, one of the first things you learn is that somebody has to clean up after them. We've got shovels, and there's a wheelbarrow behind you. When we're finished, we'll leave them food and water, and then I'll take you home. Now let's get to work."

By the time Kylie returned to the kitchen, the cookies were cool enough to decorate. She creamed the butter and powdered sugar, added a little water and a few drops of vanilla, and whipped the mixture till it was smooth and fluffy. "There," she said. "Who needs ready-made frosting?"

"But, Mom—" Amy frowned at the icing.

"What now?"

"It's *white,* Mom. These are *Christmas* cookies. We need colored icing and sprinkles."

"Oh, dear." Muriel's knitting dropped to her lap. "I haven't had sprinkles in the house for as long as I can remember. But there might be some old bottles of food coloring on the back of the spice shelf."

"I'll look." Kylie rummaged through the little

tins and jars. Toward the back corner of the shelf, she found a miniature cardboard box, like the one she remembered from her mother's kitchen a generation ago. Inside were four tiny glass bottles —red, yellow, blue, and green. One by one, she held them up to the light, with her heart sinking. All four were empty; the colored liquid was either used or dried up.

"I'm so sorry," Muriel said. "I don't know how long I've had those bottles, but I haven't used food coloring in years."

Amy gave an audible sigh, her chin sinking into her hands.

"Well, at least snow is white." Kylie was determined to be cheerful. "They can be snow cookies, and we can sprinkle a little sugar on the icing to make them sparkle. How does that sound?"

Amy gave her a dejected look. "I guess we can close our eyes when we eat them," she said.

"That's the spirit." Kylie spread a sheet of waxed paper on the table and handed her daughter a butter knife. "Let's have some fun."

Decorating the cookies didn't take long. Amy dabbed on the white icing with chilling indifference. Kylie used her fingers to sprinkle on grains of sugar. The cookies didn't look bad; but as Amy had pointed out, they didn't look much like Christmas, or even like snow, since the icing was more cream-colored than white.

Chalk up one more strikeout for Mom.

Kylie glanced at the kitchen clock. It was coming up on lunchtime, but there was no sign of the snowmobile. Maybe the machine had broken down, stranding its riders in the snow?

She should never have let Hunter go off with Shane. A short ride around the property might've been all right. But in a moment of weakness, she'd entrusted her son to one of the last men she'd have picked as a role model. Shane's bad-boy aura might seem glamorous to an impressionable youngster. However, Shane hadn't gone to college, served his country, or held down any kind of professional job. True, he'd run the family ranch for years. But all he really wanted was to bum his way around the country on a motorcycle—not the sort of life she'd planned for Hunter, and certainly not what Brad would want for his son.

Times like these were when she really missed Brad. Even when he was halfway around the world, he'd been able to talk to his family on Skype, hearing about the children's progress and making sure, in his stern but loving way, that they behaved themselves. Hunter, especially, was at an age when he needed his father and the example of duty and discipline Brad had provided. That the boy, in his father's absence, would turn to a roguish, impractical dreamer like Shane worried and frightened her.

She would need to rein Hunter in before things got out of hand.

By now, Amy had gone up to her room and Muriel had retired to her rocker by the warm fire. Kylie finished cleaning up the cookie project and had wiped the table down. She started assembling the turkey sandwiches she'd planned for lunch, along with canned beans and some potato salad. She'd be smart to make extra food. Henry would be hungry, and if Shane stuck around to work on the bike, she could hardly turn him away. Maybe later on, she'd get the chance to caution him about her son.

She was layering lettuce and sliced tomatoes over the deli meat when the snowmobile roared up to the back porch. As she stepped outside, dazzled by the brightness of sun on snow, Shane cut the engine. Spattered with snow and grinning like the happy boy she remembered, Hunter climbed off the back of the snowmobile.

"Don't track snow into the house," Kylie said. "How was the ride?"

"Awesome!" He stomped his boots on the porch. "I helped Shane shovel snow and clean the barn. It was hard, but it was fun. Shane said I was a good worker."

"I'm glad you had a good time helping," she said, sensing Shane's eyes on her. "Now go inside and get washed up for lunch. It'll be ready in a few minutes."

"Great. I'm starved." He hurried inside, leaving Kylie on the porch. She shivered under her thin pink sweater.

"You and Henry are invited for lunch, too," she said. "I made plenty of sandwiches and salad, and I'm warming up some canned beans."

"Thanks. I'll tell Henry." Shane's face was ruddy with cold; the stubble on his jaw was beaded with melting snow. He looked mouth-wateringly handsome. But this was no time to let her hormones take charge of her brain—not when the issue was his influence on her son.

"That's a fine boy you're raising," he said. "We made a good morning of it."

"I need to t-talk to you about that." Kylie's teeth had begun to chatter. Goose bumps puckered beneath her sweater.

"Sure, but right now I can tell you're freezing. Get inside. We can talk later. Go!"

Kylie ducked back into the house and closed the door. She could smell the beans she'd left warming on the back burner. They were beginning to scorch. Blast that stove!

Rushing through the kitchen, she snatched the pan off the heat. The beans would be all right as long as she was careful not to scrape the burned part off the bottom of the pan. But sometimes it seemed as if that stove hated being used by anyone other than Muriel.

At least the sandwiches would be fresh and

good. Kylie sliced each one in half and arranged them on a platter. By the time she'd ladled the beans into a bowl and put everything on the table, Shane and Henry had come inside and Muriel had awakened from her doze by the fire. "Now that looks mighty good," Henry said, holding a chair for Muriel and sliding it in as she sat down. It was a tender gesture—but did Muriel even notice such things?

"Get your sister, Hunter," Kylie said.

"Never mind, I'm coming." Amy appeared in the kitchen and took her place at the table.

There was a beat of uncertain silence before Muriel offered to say grace, and again that awkward joining of hands. It was a nice custom, really, and Kylie supposed she'd get used to it. But with Shane's big hand cocooning hers—his rough and cool, hers smooth and warm—her pulse surged into overdrive. And it didn't help that Muriel's prayer was going on and on.

". . . Lord, we thank You for keeping us safe during the storm and for our friends and family who are gathered here to enjoy this wonderful meal. . . . Bless us this holiday season that each of us will find the true meaning of Christmas in our hearts. Bless us with joy and gratitude for this day. . . . Amen."

The prayer had been a beautiful one, but with her pulse driving heat through her body, it had been all Kylie could do to concentrate on the words. As the murmured "amen" echoed around the table, she broke Shane's easy clasp and pulled away. Her cheeks were blazing. She lowered her gaze, wondering if he was looking at her, wondering if he'd noticed.

"Hey, I'm starved! Let's eat!" Hunter reached for two sandwiches and helped himself to some beans and salad. Kylie was tempted to scold him for his lack of manners, but seeing him happy was worth holding her tongue.

In a moment, they were all filling their plates. Everyone seemed hungry except Amy, who was only picking at her food. Kylie gave her a worried look. The girl was right—life wasn't fair. If only she had a reason to smile.

"You should see Shane's place!" Hunter, who was usually brooding or lost in his phone, was actually making conversation. "He's got a big barn with horses in it! And he's got a dog with four puppies—they're blue heelers. Shane says they're the best cattle dogs on the planet."

"Oh?" Kylie could imagine where this was leading.

"Shane's pups are all spoken for. But you know I've always wanted a dog. Amy too. Now that we're here on Aunt Muriel's farm, what do you say we get one?"

Kylie hesitated. A dog would be fun for her children. But right now, with so many adjustments to make, a puppy underfoot would be just one more worry. "We'll see," she said. "Maybe this spring, when the weather's better. And only then if it's all right with Aunt Muriel."

"Oh, I wouldn't mind," Muriel said. "My father always had dogs. I'd enjoy a dog now, but I'm getting too old to take care of one."

"See, Mom," Hunter argued. "It would be fine. Wouldn't it, Amy?"

"It would be great!" Amy had brightened. "Hunter and I would take care of the dog! You and Aunt Muriel wouldn't have to do a thing. Please say yes, Mom!"

"Why wait so long?" Hunter asked. "We could start looking now, online."

Kylie knew when she was being railroaded, but things were happening too fast. Dealing with the move, the storm, and trying to put Christmas together, the stress was all she could handle. The thought of puppy puddles on the floor was more than her frayed nerves could stand right now.

"We'll talk about it later," she said. "Show me that you can be responsible, help around the place, and keep your grades up. Then we'll talk about getting a dog. End of conversation."

It's what any good parent would say, Kylie told herself. But her children's eager expressions had wilted like summer flowers at the first touch of frost. She sensed Shane's eyes on her, his gaze questioning. What did he think of her?

But why should it matter? Shane had no business putting ideas into her children's heads without asking her first. The sooner she made that clear to him, the better for all concerned.

An awkward silence had fallen over the table. It was broken by a sound from the direction of the road—the grinding roar of a big machine coming closer.

Hunter was the first one out the door. "It's a bulldozer!" he shouted. "It's clearing the snow!"

"Hallelujah!" Shane came out behind him, shielding his eyes from the glare. The town fathers must've rented the machine and driver from a local construction company. It didn't cut smooth like a regular snowplow, but it was doing the job.

Behind it came a truck from the power company with a cherry picker on the back. Shane waved at the driver, a man he recognized from town. With luck they'd have the power on in the next few hours—a good thing, since the generator was running low on fuel.

He would need to clear the driveway out to the road for Henry and Kylie. That done, he'd be able to move his truck. But the snowmobile would still come in handy for the unplowed lanes and for getting around on the ranch. Maybe Henry would sell it to him.

"Maybe I can get Mom to drive me into town later," Hunter said. "Is there someplace where kids hang out?"

"There's a burger joint called Buckaroo's on the end of Main Street. It's got some arcade games in the back. But with the roads so bad, I don't think you'd find many kids hanging out there, especially two days before Christmas."

"Oh."

"Come on," Shane said. "Let's go finish our lunch. After that, if you're bored, you can help me shovel the driveway."

Hunter followed him back inside, scuffing his feet. The others were still at the table, Muriel sipping her tea, Henry spooning up the last of his beans. Amy had just set a plate of iced cookies in the center of the table. "We might as well eat them now, since they're not really Christmas cookies," she said.

"They look like Christmas to me." Shane took his seat next to Kylie and helped himself to a cookie. "They taste likc Christmas, too."

"What she means is that they're not red and green," Kylie said. "We didn't have colored icing or sprinkles. But now that the roads are clear, I could drive to Shop Mart and get some."

Shane's eyes traced her profile, lingering on the luscious lips he'd kissed last night. Kylie had always been a perfectionist, he recalled. Now she was determined to give her children a perfect

117

Christmas—and everything was working against her.

Part of him wanted to gather her in his arms, rock her like a child, and tell her to quit knocking herself out. He wanted to say that Christmas was about warmth and family and celebration, and that fancy trappings didn't matter. But something told him Kylie wouldn't listen to him. And, sadly, neither would her children.

"I wouldn't try driving if I were you," he said. "That bulldozer left a layer of packed snow on the road. With those bald tires of yours, you could slide out of control and wreck."

"You looked at my tires?"

"I gave them a passing glance. I'm surprised you made it all the way here without a blowout."

"If you need to go to town, I can drive you in my Jeep," Henry said.

"Thanks, Henry." She gave him a smile. "But you've got better things to do. I won't ask you to drive me, unless it's for something really important."

In other words, rather than impose on Henry, she'd take a chance in that rattletrap wagon on those slick tires and probably end up stuck in a ditch. Too bad her vehicle was parked in the shed; otherwise, he could "accidentally" bury it in snow.

Shane rose from his chair. "I'll take another cookie. Then I'll be off to shovel the driveway. No need to help me, Henry. I don't want you throwing your back out like you did last winter."

"Maybe you should invest in a snowblower," Kylie said.

"Hardly worth it when a storm like this only happens once every few years. We're tough here in Texas. We can shovel. Thanks for lunch, ladies—and for dessert." Shane slid another cookie off the plate, lifted his coat off the chair, and walked outside.

There were two shovels by the porch and a wide expanse of snow to clear off the driveway. Shane was hoping Hunter might come out and help him, but he didn't show up. Maybe his mother needed him for something. Or maybe the boy was just tired.

He'd resolved not to get involved with Kylie and her children, Shane reminded himself. But it was already happening. It had started when he'd kissed Kylie last night—a brief, innocent kiss that had rocked his senses in a way he couldn't forget. Then this morning, he'd gotten to know Hunter, and to like the boy. Now he was concerned about the drivability of Kylie's car and her safety on the road.

He jammed the shovel under the snow and tossed the load to one side. Damn it, he was getting sucked in—and he wasn't happy about it. He'd wanted to sell the ranch and make a clean break from Branding Iron, Texas, with nothing to call him back. Later on, if he got tired of being on the road, he could always settle down, but it wouldn't be here. It would be someplace wild and beautiful, like the backcountry of Wyoming or the Pacific Northwest.

Anyplace but here, where he'd always been—and always would be—a loner with a shadowed past.

His memory drifted back to the week his mother had died. His father had insisted he go back to high school the day after her funeral, and Shane had obeyed. But he'd been hurting with a gut-deep grief so painful that the only ease for it had been doing something to make his wretched life even worse.

Once decided, the rest had been easy. Like someone with a death wish, he'd walked up to the biggest, toughest guy in school, class president and all-state quarterback Ben Marsden. Standing tall and looking into Ben's steely eyes, he'd delivered the worst possible slur about the cheerleader Ben was dating.

When Ben's sledgehammer fist crashed into his jaw, Shane had welcomed the pain. His refusal to take back what he'd said had earned him another blow, then another. At first he'd willed himself not to fight back. But then his anger had blazed, and he began trading punch for punch, doing some serious damage to Ben's movie-star face. By now, a yelling, cheering crowd had gathered, most of them rooting for Ben.

By the time the coach and the principal rushed in to drag them apart, both boys were staggering like drunkards. They'd ended up sitting side by side in the principal's office, both of them stonily silent, each too proud to blame the other.

Both of them had been sent home with a week's suspension. Shane had taken off on his motor-cycle, lifted a six-pack of beer from the local convenience store, driven down to his spot on the river and drunk himself senseless. When he'd recovered enough to go home and face his grieving father, he'd vowed that, as soon as he turned eighteen, he would leave Branding Iron and never look back.

He hadn't, of course. His father had needed him, and so he'd stayed. But there was a wild part of him that had never been tied to this town or to the ranch that was now his. That part of him, like a caged hawk yearning to fly, had always yearned to be free.

Soon, Shane told himself, he would be.

Chapter Seven

Kylie turned away from the sink, where she'd finished washing the dishes from lunch. "Stay here, Hunter. I need to talk to you."

Hunter had taken the old plaid coat off the back

of the chair and was slipping one arm into a sleeve. "Can't it wait? I need to help Shane shovel snow."

"Shane will be fine. Sit down." They were alone in the kitchen. Henry had gone outside. Amy had gone back to her room, and Muriel was dozing by the fireplace in her rocker.

"I don't get it." Hunter took a seat, still holding the coat. "You wanted me to show some responsibility. That's what I'm trying to do."

"I know." Kylie dried her hands on a dish towel. She wasn't looking forward to this discussion. But disappointing her son now would be less cruel than having his young heart crushed later on, when Shane let him down.

"You had fun this morning, didn't you?" She pulled out a chair and sat across the table from him.

"Yeah, I had a great time." He eyed her suspiciously. "What's wrong? I asked you. You said I could go."

"Yes, I did. And no, you haven't done anything wrong. I'm just a little worried, that's all."

"What about?" The furrow that deepened between his eyebrows reminded Kylie of the way Brad had looked when he was displeased.

"You still miss your father, don't you?"

"Sure I do. It's kind of like when he was deployed, except that we can't Skype and we know he's not coming back. It sucks. But what's that got to do with now?"

122

Kylie's gaze dropped to her hands. So far, Hunter was making more sense than she was. But this was no time to back off and start over. She needed to voice her concerns.

"What do you think of Shane?" she asked. "Do you think he's a good role model for a young boy?"

Hunter's frown deepened. A spark of defiance flickered in his hazel eyes. "Is that what this is about, Mom? You don't want me hanging out with Shane?"

"It's just that I remember what he was like in high school. He still rides that old motorcycle, and who knows what else he still does? I can't imagine—"

"He's not like that," Hunter interrupted. "Shane's cool. He told me he did some stupid things when he was young, but he's learned better, and he doesn't want me to make the same mistakes. He even told me to listen to my mother. He said you were smart and knew what was best. Sheesh!"

"Fine." Kylie bit back any further words about Shane's character. With her son's defenses up, there'd be no changing his mind. But she had another, deeper concern.

"Shane's planning to leave, you know," she said. "As soon as he finds a buyer for his ranch, he'll turn his back on Branding Iron and be off to roam the country."

"He already told me that, Mom."

"The two of you must've had quite a talk."

"We did, while we were working. What's wrong with that?"

"Nothing. It's just that . . ." Kylie hesitated. How could she speak her mind without sounding judgmental and overprotective?

"I know you've missed having a man in your life," she said. "But you're still getting over the loss of your dad. I don't want to see you get attached to Shane and be hurt all over again when he leaves. And he *will* leave. He's wanted to get away from Branding Iron for as long as I've known him."

Hunter's fingers twisted a button on the old plaid coat. His young face wore a pained expression. "Stop treating me like a baby, Mom," he said. "I've had to grow up a lot since Dad died. I know all about losing people and stuff like that. If Shane rides off into the sunset, like in the movie, I can handle it fine."

"But why a man like Shane? You'll be starting school in a couple of weeks. You'll have plenty of friends your own age."

"Get off my case, Mom!" The burst of temper came without warning. "I'm not five years old anymore! I don't need you protecting me all the time! Damn it, you're driving me crazy!"

Frozen in momentary shock, Kylie stared at her son. "Since when do you curse at your mother like that?" she demanded. "Where did you learn that? From Shane?"

"Mom—"

"No, not another word. Give me your cell phone, then go straight to your room. You're in time-out till I say so!"

"*Time-out!* See what I mean? You're still treating me like a baby!" Standing, Hunter slammed his phone on the table, almost—but not quite—hard enough to break it. Then he turned and stormed off toward the stairs.

Fighting tears, Kylie slumped over the table. Her son was so young and vulnerable and trying so hard to be a man. She would do anything to protect him. But today wisdom had failed her. She'd wanted to keep him close, but she'd only pushed him away. Maybe she was the one who needed a time-out.

In a nervous gesture, her fingers twisted her gold wedding band. When Brad was alive, he'd spent far more time away than at home. She'd pretty much raised the children on her own, but his unseen presence had always been there, his quiet discipline a guidepost for them all. Now he was gone and their children were growing into adolescence, changing into emotional young strangers before her eyes. She'd hoped that a perfect Christmas would make up for having their lives uprooted. But something told her even that wouldn't be enough—and this holiday was turning out to be one long string of disasters.

From the yard outside, she could hear the scrape of Shane's shovel as he cleared the snow off the long driveway. Shane was part of her problem with Hunter, she reminded herself. Letting him know where she stood might be a step, at least, toward some kind of resolution.

Muriel's quilted down coat hung on a rack by the door. Surely, Muriel wouldn't mind if she borrowed it. Kylie lifted it off the hook and slipped it on. The sleeves were a couple of inches too short, but at least it would be warmer than her thin fleece jacket. Zipping up the front, Kylie stepped out onto the porch.

The whiteness of sunlight on snow was dazzling. Kylie shaded her eyes with one hand as she closed the door behind her. From part-way down the drive, Shane, wearing sunglasses, paused in his shoveling to look back at her. "Hi," he said. "Where's Hunter? I was hoping he'd come out and give me a hand."

"Sorry, he's in time-out." Kylie's breath vaporized in puffs on the winter air. "I sent him to his room for mouthing off to his mother."

"*Mouthing off?* That doesn't sound like Hunter. He strikes me as a respectful kid."

Kylie took a deep breath. "That's something we need to discuss." She took the spare shovel from where it leaned against the house. "I'll help you shovel while we talk."

"You're sure? You don't have gloves. You'll freeze your hands."

"That won't matter, I . . . Wait, there's something here."

Kylie shoved her hands into the deep pockets of Muriel's coat and found two worn, faded wool gloves. It took a little stretching to pull them over her long fingers, but they'd do for now. And she'd worn warm socks under her sneakers. As long as she stood on shoveled ground, her feet would be fine.

"Here goes." With a little grunt of effort, she scooped a mound of heavy snow. She could feel the strain in her back and shoulders as she hefted it and tossed it to one side.

"Did that hurt?" he asked.

"It's been a few years."

"I can imagine." Shane flashed her a movie-star smile. "Tell you what. I'll go ahead of you and break the path. You can follow me and scoop up the loose snow I leave behind."

"I think you're babying me," Kylie said.

He laughed. "Just want to make sure you'll be able to straighten up tomorrow. Not so sure about myself. But come on, let's try it."

Shane's idea turned out to be a practical one. For the first few minutes, they worked in silence. Shane tossed the heavy snow to one side, and

Kylie scraped a clean path behind him while she worked up the nerve to open up what was bound to be a touchy subject.

Finally it was Shane who spoke. "You said you had something to discuss."

"That's right." Kylie hesitated, suddenly uncertain. With Hunter she'd tried to clear the air and managed to leave the situation in shambles. Would she do the same with Shane?

"Let me guess." He flung another mound of snow off the side of the drive. "You're uneasy because your son spent the morning with me, and you're not sure it was a good idea."

He'd taken the offensive, leaving her speechless, but only for the space of a breath. "He swore at me, Shane. He's never done that before."

"Well, I promise you, he didn't learn that from me."

"Oh, I'm sure he's picked up swearwords from other boys. But he's never used one to my face. It's as if he came home with a whole new attitude."

"And you're blaming that on me?"

"I don't know." She was stumbling now. "But I do know he needs a man in his life, someone he can look up to as a role model."

"And you don't think I'm the man for the job." He'd stopped shoveling and was looking down at her with a mocking smile on his lips. "That makes sense. The Shane Taggart you remember was a troublemaker and a rule breaker, and he's still tearing around on that old Harley—or *was,* until you wrecked it."

"I said I was sorry, and that my insurance would pay."

"I know. And I understand that I'm not the ideal role model for your boy. So, have you got somebody else in mind? I never bothered to ask, did I?"

Heat flamed in Kylie's face. She managed to find her voice. "It's not that. But right now, to hear Hunter talk, it's like you hung the moon. He's still dealing with his father's loss. I don't want him hurt when you leave here, Shane. The boy's been through enough."

Shane's smile had faded. The dark sunglasses masked his eyes, reflecting Kylie's image back at her. "Hunter's a good kid," he said. "I wouldn't hurt him for the world. If you want me to keep my distance, I'll respect your wishes. But understand that I'll be spending time here, helping Henry and working on the bike. If you don't want Hunter around me, it'll be your job to keep him away."

"Oh, I know he'll be interested in the bike, and in helping Henry. Just . . . don't try to influence him, okay? Don't take him anywhere or treat him like anything special. That's all I'm asking. I just don't want him hurt."

"I get the message." Shane thrust the shovel hard into the snow. "But I want Hunter to understand why I won't be his friend anymore. That'll be up to you."

She felt his coldness like an icy wind, penetrating to her bones. "Of course. Don't worry, I'll handle it," she said.

"Fine. And now that you've said what you came to say, you can put that shovel down and go back in the house. Go on, before you freeze. I don't need your help."

"All right. As long as we understand each other." Kylie stuck her shovel upright in the snow. Stripping off the gloves and stuffing them back into the pockets of Muriel's coat, she turned and strode back toward the porch. Her eyes stung, but not from the cold or the glare. All she'd wanted was to protect her son, as any good mother would. But had she done the right thing? Or had her clumsy efforts only made the situation worse?

Shane had surely meant well, taking Hunter under his wing. But he was a proud man, and her implication that he was a bad influence must have stung. It wasn't really what she'd meant, but she could imagine how her words had struck him.

Part of her wanted to turn around, walk back to Shane, and apologize to him. But that would only complicate things. What was done was done, and would be safer left alone.

Returning to the house, she noticed the hum of the generator had stopped. She flipped the switch on the back porch light. The light came on. The power outage appeared to be over. At least that was something to be grateful for.

She slipped off Muriel's coat and hung it on the hook, where she'd found it. Muriel and Amy were seated at the kitchen table with a big flat cardboard box, still taped shut, between them.

"Look, Mom!" Amy's blue eyes danced. "I found this in the pile of stuff we haven't unpacked yet. It's our Christmas box!"

Kylie recognized the box at once and knew what was inside. Every year of her marriage to Brad, she'd purchased a special ceramic ornament for their tree—a pair of wedding bells the first year, a blue baby angel for the year of Hunter's birth, and a pink one for Amy's. For the years in between, there were cars and airplanes, a miniature house, a Santa in army camouflage.

Last year there'd been nothing. Nor would there be this year. There was no time and no place to buy a new ornament. But then, there was also no tree.

Kylie had packed each precious ornament in Bubble Wrap, along with a few other decorations that were her children's favorites. In the craziness of post-move stress, she'd almost forgotten about them. But Amy hadn't.

"Amy wanted to show me these ornaments," Muriel said. "She says they all have stories. I can't wait to hear each one."

"I know we don't have a tree yet." Amy was tearing at the tape that held the box shut. "But maybe if we get the decorations out, it'll feel more like Christmas. Besides, we might still get a tree."

"There's always my old silver one in the attic," Muriel said.

"No, I want a real tree, one that will make the whole house smell like Christmas. I'm going to wish and wish till it happens."

An ache stirred in Kylie's throat. Amy had gone through the same process when Brad was killed—she'd tried and tried to wish her father back. But it hadn't happened, of course. Now her precious daughter was about to get her hopes crushed again—unless, by some miracle, they could find a tree.

Amy wadded up the sticky tape and opened the flaps of the box. With eager hands, she picked up an ornament and unwound the Bubble Wrap.

"Oh no!" she wailed. "It's broken!"

Kylie had been about to start dinner, but her daughter's cry brought her rushing to the table. The little camouflage Santa lay on the Bubble Wrap, broken in three pieces—head, body, and legs. Tears were welling in Amy's eyes.

"I've got glue," Muriel said. "We can fix it."

"Let's check the others first." Kylie began lifting the Bubble-Wrapped ornaments out of the box. She'd tried to stow it in a safe place, but things had evidently shifted during the long trip to Texas. Something heavy had crushed the box. More than half the precious ornaments were broken.

Amy had begun to cry—little hiccupping sobs that tore at Kylie's heart. Muriel rose, rummaged through a drawer, and came up with a tube of glue.

"Here, Amy," she said, sitting down again. "This is good glue. I've used it to mend china dishes. We can fix these as good as new."

"They'll never be as good as new!" Amy dabbed at her nose with a tissue.

"Watch." Muriel picked up the body of the Santa; she unstoppered the tube and squeezed a thin trail of glue along the broken edge of the neck. "One thing you'll learn by the time you're my age, my sweet girl, is that not many things in life stay good as new. Mostly, you have to mend them—or if they're not worth mending, you throw them away and move on. Remember that as you grow up."

With deft fingers, she placed the head of the little Santa onto the thread of glue, making an almost invisible seam. "Now hold that till it sets." She handed the piece to Amy and picked up the broken legs. Amy had stopped crying and was watching her apply the glue. "Pay attention to how it's done," she said. "Then you can try the next one."

Kylie turned back to scrubbing potatoes for baking with the meat loaf she'd mixed earlier. She'd assumed she was coming here to look after a failing old woman. How could she have imagined the lessons her great-aunt Muriel would teach her?

"What's the temperature for meat loaf and potatoes?" she asked.

"Three-fifty should do it," Muriel said. "Put in enough for Henry. He'll be hungry after working in the cold."

And Shane? But Kylie knew better than to ask. Even as she thought of him, the sound of shoveling stopped. A moment later, she heard his pickup roar to life and drive away.

The plowed road was slippery with packed snow. But the pickup had four-wheel drive and good tires. Shane had no trouble making it back to the graveled lane that cut off to his ranch. From here the going would be slower. But the earlier run with the snowmobile had broken a track. Gearing down, he eased the truck forward.

The crawling pace and the white silence outside gave his mind the freedom to wander—too much freedom, given where his thoughts took him. He'd already replayed the confrontation with Kylie too many times. The last thing he wanted was to go there again.

Kylie might be a widow and a mother, but some

things never changed. Little Miss Perfect still thought she was too good for him—and that he was a bad influence on her son. Except for the children involved, it was like high school all over again. He'd given up his wild ways, run the ranch for his father, and earned the respect of most people in Branding Iron. But to Kylie none of that counted. He was still the boy who'd gotten busted for stealing a beer from a convenience store and never lived it down.

Well, what of it? He didn't need her approval. He would go about his business, be distantly polite to her and her children, and hope the sale of the ranch would soon set him free. He would miss Henry and Muriel; but with Kylie there, and a boy who was getting strong enough to help with chores, they should be fine.

Up ahead he could see the house and out-buildings. Everything looked peaceful. He'd fed the animals that morning, so he could wait a little to go out to the barn. Right now, his first priority was the house. Now that the power was on, he needed to get some heat in the place, check the pipes, and open his e-mail.

Maybe he ought to phone Holly back. A few drinks and a mindless roll in the sack might help him forget his troubles with Kylie for a few hours. But it would be, at best, a temporary fix—the sort of fix that would prove what Kylie *had* implied about him was true. In the long run, seeing Holly would only make things worse.

Since there wasn't much he could do to avoid Kylie, he would just have to be polite to her and keep his distance from her kids. Too bad about that. He was getting to know and like Hunter and Amy. But now that he knew where he stood with their mother, the sooner he could pack up and leave, the better.

When he turned up the thermostat, the furnace responded with a blast of warmth, which prompted him to take off his coat. The pipes, too, were all right. In the alcove that served as a home office, Shane sat down at the desk, switched on his computer, and brought up his e-mail.

Few of his messages were worth reading. He scrolled down, deleting most, until he came to one that caught his eye. It was from Helen Floyd, an old friend of his mother's. After her husband's death, Helen had become a real estate broker. Shane had listed his ranch with her, not only because of the friendship, but because Helen was a sharp saleswoman who knew how to use nationwide Internet marketing.

Hi, Shane, I just may have found a buyer for your ranch. A couple from Michigan took the photo tour and contacted me. The wife has fallen in love with your Craftsman home, especially the view from the front with those stately pines flanking the porch. The husband likes the investment potential and having a place where their family could ride horses most of the year. I did some checking. They're financially solid and shouldn't have a problem raising the cash. They want to fly down after the holidays and take a look. If they like the place, they'll make you an offer. Keep your fingers crossed, Helen

Shane stared at the computer screen, his heart thudding in the stillness of the empty house. This outcome was what he'd wanted, what he'd planned for since his father's passing. He should be doing handsprings down the hall. What he felt, instead, was a sense of unreality. He'd lived his whole life on this ranch, sweated and bled for it, cared for it, hated it, loved it.

Maybe the sale would fall through.

But what was he thinking? If these people didn't buy the ranch, somebody else would. He had to face the reality of what was going to happen. If he wanted to be free, he had to prepare himself to let go.

Only now did he realize how painful that letting go might be.

Outside, the setting sun had turned the clouds to fire. Hues of flame, saffron, violet, and indigo streaked across the sky, reflecting soft rose gold on the quiet snow. Standing at the window, Shane watched the colors deepen and fade. Then he slipped on his coat and walked out to the barn to take care of his animals.

While the meat loaf and potatoes baked in the oven, Kylie sat at the table and helped Amy and Muriel mend the broken ornaments. Lost in the delicate task, Amy had forgotten her tears. The little figures were coming together nicely.

"See, I told you we could fix them," Muriel said. "The secret is to know what you're doing, and to do it carefully."

"And they do look *almost* as good as new," Amy said. "They'll be nice enough for the Christmas tree—when we get a Christmas tree." She turned to her mother. "I was thinking, Mom, we could have Shane take us out on the snowmobile. We could find a pine tree, cut it down, and drag it home. That's how people got Christmas trees in the old days, isn't it, Aunt Muriel?"

"Well, yes," Muriel said. "But things have changed since I was a little girl. These days, if we cut down a tree on somebody's property, we could get in trouble. Sadly, all the land around here is somebody's property."

And, thanks to your mother, Shane won't be taking anybody out on the snowmobile.

Kylie kept that comment to herself. She'd already begun to regret her clumsily spoken words. But Shane would remember them, and he would keep his proud distance.

Amy worked in silence for a moment, pressing a wing onto the miniature airplane and holding it steady so the glue would set. "How come you never got married, Aunt Muriel?" Amy asked. "You must've been pretty."

She is still pretty, Kylie thought, *like a dainty little silver bird.*

"My goodness!" Muriel sounded flustered. "I thought we were talking about Christmas trees. Where did that question come from?"

"I just wanted to know," Amy said. "So, how come you didn't?"

"Well, for one thing, my father was sick and I had to take care of him."

"And why else?"

"Maybe . . ." Muriel paused, lost in thought. "Maybe because the right man never asked me."

"Well"—Amy set the airplane on the table—"I was thinking you could marry Henry. He's old like you and he's nice. If you got married, he could live in the house with us, and not in that old trailer. Maybe you could ask him."

Muriel's pale cheeks flushed pink. "Heavens, child, where did you come up with that idea? In my day, it was always the man who did the asking—and I'm still an old-fashioned girl!" She sniffed the kitchen air, as if scrambling for a diversion. "Goodness, I do believe the meat loaf and potatoes are done. Let's clear this project away and set the table for dinner. We can finish later."

Kylie put the mended treasures and the glue in the box and put it in an out-of-the-way corner. "Amy and I can set the table," Muriel said, rising. "Kylie, maybe you can go out and tell Henry it's almost ready. Where's Hunter?"

"He's in his room. He said you gave him time-out." Amy was carrying five plates to the table. "Can I tell him to come down and eat, Mom?"

"Finish setting the table. Then you can go get him." Her son had been punished long enough, Kylie decided. If he apologized, he might even get his phone back.

Slipping on Muriel's coat, she went out the back door and followed the shoveled path to the machine shed. She found Henry gazing morosely down at an array of bent, broken motorcycle pieces spread out on the concrete floor.

Guilt punched her like a giant fist, but she decided not to ask questions.

"Muriel sent me out here to invite you in to dinner," she said. "It's almost ready."

A smile flickered across his face. "She didn't need to do that. I've got TV dinners I can heat up in the microwave."

"Not tonight. Your place is already set at the table. I hope you like meat loaf."

"You bet I do."

"Then I'll see you inside. Don't be too long."

Leaving him, Kylie hurried back to the house. By now, it was getting dark, the sunset no more than a pale streak above the western horizon. Tomorrow would be Christmas Eve, and she had nothing for the children, no tree and no presents. What was she going to do?

As she entered the kitchen, Amy came down the stairs, worry written all over her face.

"What's the matter?" Kylie asked, alarmed. "Where's Hunter?"

"He wasn't in his room or anywhere upstairs," Amy said. "I can't find him anywhere, and his coat is gone. Mom, I think he's run away."

It took seconds for the words to penetrate. Then it was as if the air had been sucked from Kylie's body and replaced by an awful dread. It was almost dark, and deadly cold outside. Hunter wasn't used to the weather, and those old borrowed clothes and boots he had on weren't all that warm. If he was out there now, he could be in real danger—and it was all her fault. If she hadn't pushed him about Shane and ruined the only good time he'd had since his arrival here, he wouldn't have talked back to her. She wouldn't have given him time out, and he wouldn't be gone now.

"Maybe he's just holed up somewhere," Henry said. "I'll take the flashlight and check the sheds. I'll check my trailer, too. At least he'd be warm in there."

Muriel handed him the flashlight. "Be careful.

It's icy out there. You could slip in the dark."

"I'll go with Henry," Kylie said, sensing Muriel's worry about the old man. "Amy, you search upstairs. Look anywhere he might be, even the attic. Muriel, you might want to wait here in case somebody calls us."

"All right. I can't do much more except say a little prayer."

Dinner forgotten, they scattered to look for Hunter. Shivering in Muriel's quilted coat, Kylie steadied Henry's arm as they went down the steps and crossed the yard. The machine shed had a light. Henry slid the door open and switched it on. Everything was quiet. There was no sign of Hunter.

In the vehicle shed, they shone the light into Kylie's station wagon and Henry's Jeep. They found nothing there, and nothing in Henry's trailer.

"I'm getting scared," Kylie said as they walked back toward the house. Her feet felt like ice lumps in her thin sneakers. "What if he's lost? What if he's freezing?"

"Hunter's a strong boy, and he's not a fool," Henry said. "I know you're worried, but he'll be fine."

"Thanks, Henry, I hope so." Kylie knew the old man was trying to calm her fear, but his words weren't enough. Forcing her cold-muddled brain to concentrate, she tried to put herself in Hunter's place. If she was an angry young boy who'd been punished by his mother, where would she go?

Only one answer made sense.

Chapter Eight

Shane had settled down with a cold beer to watch the evening news when the phone rang. He was surprised to see Kylie's name on the caller ID display. Earlier that day, she'd behaved as if she never wanted to talk to him again.

"What's up, Kylie?" He tried to sound casual.

"It's Hunter." He could hear the strain in her voice. "He's missing. We've looked everywhere for him, even in the sheds and in Henry's trailer. Could he be at your place?"

"I haven't seen him. Have you tried calling his cell phone?"

"I took his phone away to punish him. He doesn't have it."

Shane took a breath to weigh what he'd heard. He'd only meant to be kind, befriending Kylie's son. But if he'd left well enough alone, the boy might not be missing now. "I'll take a look around and call you back," he said, rising. "Okay?"

"Yes. Thanks." She drew a ragged breath. "I don't know how long he's been gone. He was upset when I sent him to his room this afternoon, but we didn't realize he'd left until dinnertime. Shane, it's so cold out there, and Hunter's a California boy. He doesn't understand the danger.

If he's in trouble somewhere, he could freeze."

"I'll check the barn. He liked the pups I have out there. Maybe he's with them. Hang on, I'll call you back."

Flinging on his sheepskin coat and grabbing a flashlight, he strode outside. It was almost five miles from Muriel's to his place. Men and animals had been known to die from the brutal cold that followed a blue norther. If Kylie's son had made it to the barn, he'd likely be all right. But if he'd fallen down on the way or stopped to rest . . .

Shane didn't want to finish the thought. Hunter had to be found before it was too late.

It was dark by now. Through the trees, a paper-thin crescent moon etched patterns of light and shadow across the snow. Shane followed the shoveled path to the barn. He found the animals undisturbed, with no sign of the boy anywhere.

Back inside the house, he called Kylie again. "He's not here. Stay put. I'm heading to your place in the truck. I'll take it slow and check both sides of the road. If he's out there, I'll find him."

"Thanks." She paused, her breathing sharp and shallow over the phone. "I'm worried sick. Hunter's never done anything like this."

"We'll find him, Kylie. If he shows up, call my cell. I'll do the same for you." Shane ended the call, got his keys from the house, and then started the pickup. The moon didn't give much light, but the snow was diamond white. If Hunter was anywhere near the road, it shouldn't be too hard to spot him.

He drove less than fifteen miles an hour, his eyes scanning the white road ahead and the snowy landscape on either side. He could imagine what Kylie must be feeling. She'd already lost her husband. To lose her son, too, would be unthinkable. But that didn't mean it couldn't happen.

In the distance now, he could see the lights of Muriel's house. Eyes searching, Shane drove at a crawl, but there was no sign of Hunter.

Kylie was waiting in the yard, with Muriel's quilted coat clutched tight against the cold. Her frightened eyes met Shane's through the side window. He shook his head and reached across to open the door on the passenger side.

"No sign of him? No tracks even?" Her teeth were chattering as she climbed in and turned in the seat to face him.

"Nothing. I searched every inch along that road. Is there anywhere else he might've gone?"

She gave a little lift of her shoulders. "Not that I—"

"Wait!" Shane's fist thumped the dash as he remembered. "He asked me if there was someplace in town where kids went to hang out. I told him there was a burger joint with arcade games. It's called Buckaroo's."

"You told him that? And you didn't think he'd try to get there?"

"Hell, the place is ten miles away. And with two feet of snow on the ground—"

"You don't know Hunter. His middle name should be 'Determination.' " She turned away from him, reached for her seat belt, and fastened it with an angry click. "Let's go."

"Hang on a minute. I want to check for tracks." Shane shifted into neutral and left the engine running to warm the cab. Taking his flashlight, he climbed to the ground and knelt to inspect the shoveled drive. It took him a few minutes to find the prints of what he knew to be Hunter's old rubber boots. They were leading out toward the road.

"Find anything?" she asked as he climbed back into the cab.

"You know your boy, all right. Looks like he was headed for the road to town." Shane fastened his seat belt and put the truck in gear.

"But how could he expect to make it that far, in this cold, without freezing?" Her voice held a mother's terror.

"Hunter's a smart kid. He'd have sense enough to know he couldn't walk that far. But people have been driving into town since the road was plowed. It wouldn't have been that hard for him to hitch a ride."

"*Hitch a ride?* But Hunter's never been allowed

to hitchhike! We need to call nine-one-one! He could've been grabbed by some predator, some monster who'd—"

"Relax," Shane said. "This isn't California. There are plenty of good folks out here who'd stop and give a boy a ride to town and not think twice about it. The kind of predator you're talking about would find pickings mighty slim around here, especially since anybody who harmed a youngster would be tracked down by a posse of armed citizens."

"You'd better be right!" With a little huffing sound, she settled back into her seat.

"We're going to find your boy and he'll be fine," Shane said. "I can feel it in my bones."

"Or maybe you're just feeling a touch of what Muriel calls 'rheumatism.' "

Her wry humor tugged at Shane's heart. Under that fussy, perfectionist exterior was a woman of amazing courage, he reminded himself. She'd been through living hell and was still holding her spunky little head high, struggling to keep her wounded family safe and happy.

"I've been wanting to apologize for what I told you earlier," she said. "I didn't mean it the way it sounded."

"You were just being protective. I understood." It was only a half-truth. At the time, her words had stung like lye. But now, seeing her fear and concern, he knew better. She was like a feisty little mother cat, defending her kittens against all comers. And he'd felt the prick of her claws.

They were on the main road now. Shane drove at a crawl. The frozen surface was slick. He didn't want to slide, and he didn't want to miss any sign of Hunter.

"Keep your eyes open," he told her. "Watch for tracks or anything else that might help."

"You don't have to tell me. I've been watching the whole time."

"Of course you have. Sorry."

"It's all right. If you had children of your own, you'd understand."

"I'm trying to, Kylie."

There was a beat of silence. "I'm scared," she said.

"Me too." Without taking his eyes off the road, Shane reached out with his free right hand, meaning to give her a comforting pat on the shoulder. But it was her soft, cool cheek his fingers brushed. He hadn't meant his touch to be a caress, but that's what it was. He felt her quiver, heard the slight catch of her breath before he moved his hand away.

They stayed quiet a moment, both of them sharply aware of each other's presence. "What if he isn't there?" she asked.

"Then we'll keep looking, or call the sheriff if we have to. But don't think about that now. We'll find him."

They were coming into town now. It was barely eight o'clock, but Main Street was quiet. Most stores and shops were already closed. At the main intersection, colored Christmas lights, strung between the power poles, blinked on and off in the dark.

Banks of plowed snow lined the street, spilling onto the sidewalks. Traffic was light, mostly headed out of town or toward the new strip mall on the outskirts. A wandering mutt lifted its leg on a half-buried fire hydrant and scampered out of sight.

"Where's the burger place?" Kylie asked.

"At the end of the street, around the corner. They're open till ten on weeknights, midnight on Friday and Saturday."

"Sounds like you might spend a little time there."

"I do, when I get tired of my own cooking. They make pretty good cheeseburgers."

Shane could feel the rise in tension as they rounded the corner. Light from the flashing blue neon sign—a cartoon cowboy on a bucking horse—flooded the cab as they pulled into the Buckaroo's parking lot. Shane noticed at once that they weren't there alone. A half-dozen big road bikes were lined up along the curb.

He pulled into a spot and braked. Kylie gave him a wide-eyed glance. "Stay put. I'll check this out," he told her.

"What if Hunter's in there with those . . . bikers?"

"Let's hope he is. Whoever they are, those boys have their own rules of conduct. They'd never hurt a kid."

Leaving the heater running, Shane climbed out of the cab and walked into the café. The bikers, tough-looking men in thick leather coats, bandannas, and navy-style watch caps, were at the bar wolfing down burgers and fries. Slim, who owned the place, was behind the bar, refilling mugs of hot coffee. Shane glanced back toward the shadowed booths. There was no sign of Hunter.

"Howdy." The nearest biker, a burly man with a scruffy, carrot-colored beard, gave Shane a friendly nod. "There's a spare stool at the far end if you need to sit."

"Thanks, but I don't plan to be here long," Shane said. "Mighty cold night for you boys to be on the road."

The biker swigged his coffee. "We need to make Amarillo by morning. Our good buddy up that way bought it when a semi driver changed lanes and didn't see him. His funeral's tomorrow. We aim to be there to carry out his coffin and ride behind it to the cemetery."

"You've got a long, cold ride ahead of you," Shane said. "Here's wishing you a safe trip. Sorry about your friend."

The big man shrugged. "Reckon it was his time. What brings you out on a night like this?"

"I'm looking for a boy," Shane said. "About thirteen, sandy hair, wearing an old plaid coat. Any of you seen him?"

Slim glanced up from refilling the coffee machine. "A boy like that was here. A truck let him off in the parking lot a couple of hours ago. He came inside, bought a Coke and said he was waiting for his friends. I let him hang out in a booth. He was here for quite a spell, but I don't see him now."

"I seen that kid." One of the bikers spoke up. "He was here when we came in. The little mutt took one look at us, hightailed it into the men's room, and locked himself in a stall. Far as I know, he's still there."

"Thanks." Shane strode down the hall to the men's restroom. He stepped inside and closed the door behind him. There were three stalls; two were open. One was closed, but there were no feet showing below the door.

"Hunter, it's Shane. Are you in here?" Shane kept his voice low and cautious.

A pair of rubber boots appeared below the edge of the door and descended to the concrete floor. The lock on the stall clicked open. Hunter, looking scared and sheepish, stepped out. "Are those bikers gone?" he asked.

"They're still here, but they won't bother you.

Come on, your mother's waiting outside in the truck. She's been worried about you. We all have."

He took a step; then he hesitated. "Shane?"

"What is it?"

"Could you please not tell Mom that I got scared and hid? I don't want her to know her son's a coward."

Shane gave him a smile. "You're not a coward. Hey, those guys do look pretty scary."

"Promise you won't tell her?"

"I promise. Now let's go."

The bikers were still at the bar. As Shane and Hunter emerged from the hall, the man with the orange beard rose and lumbered toward them. He was built like a bear; his smile showed a gap where a tooth had been. "Howdy, son," he boomed, addressing Hunter. "Bill's the name. Pleased to meet you. I've got a boy about your age, but he's with his mother. I haven't seen him in a long time. How's about a high five?" He extended his huge paw of a hand, fingers raised and spread. After a second's hesitation, Hunter gave him a hand smack. By then, the boy was grinning, no longer scared.

"It's a cold night to be out," Bill said. "You ought to be mighty glad your dad came and found you."

"He's not . . . ," Hunter began, but then broke off. "Let's go, Dad," he said, motioning Shane toward the door.

Dad. Nobody had ever called Shane that. Even if it wasn't true, the word warmed a hidden spot he'd been unaware of until now. As he followed Hunter out the door, he glanced back at Bill. "You boys have a safe trip."

"Thanks," the big biker said. "And you take good care of your boy. He's a fine one, and kids are mighty precious. Believe me, I know."

With a farewell nod, Shane followed his temporary son outside into the freezing dark. As soon as she saw them, Kylie flung open the door, sprang out of the truck, and snatched her errant boy into her arms.

"You are in so much trouble, Hunter Wayne!" she said. But there was no mistaking the fierce mother love in her voice. "Do you want to talk about this now or in the morning?"

"In the morning, please." He yawned. "I'm so tired."

Shane opened the door to the bench seat in the back of the cab. "There's an old quilt in here. Cover up and get some rest if you want."

Without a word, Hunter crawled onto the seat, found the quilt, and made a cocoon of it. By the time Shane had closed Kylie's door and gone around to climb into the driver's seat, he was already asleep.

Kylie glanced back at her slumbering son. Filling her eyes with the sight of him, she breathed a prayer of thanks. If the worst had happened tonight, she could have lost him. But he was here. He was safe.

How could she have managed without Shane, whose help had made all the difference? It would be so easy to fall into his arms and weep with relief. But even if he hadn't been driving, that would be a bad idea. Shane Taggart was a one-way ticket to heartbreak. The sooner she got that through her head, the better.

Her nerves were still wound tight. As Shane turned off Main Street onto the road for home, she leaned back in the seat and tried to relax. Falling into her old habit, she went to twist her gold wedding ring.

Her heart dropped. Where the ring had been for fourteen years, she felt nothing except a band of smooth-worn skin.

"Oh . . ." She gave a little moan.

Shane glanced at her. "Are you all right?"

"No." Her heart was pounding. "My wedding ring—it's gone."

There was a beat of startled silence. "You're saying you've lost it?"

"I never take it off, day or night. But after all the things I've done today"—she paused, going down her mental list—"making cookies, shoveling snow, peeling potatoes, washing dishes . . . somehow it must've slipped off. And now it's—it's *gone*."

"It isn't gone, Kylie. Your ring has to be somewhere. With any luck at all, it'll turn up."

"That's easy for you to say. My luck's been running pretty low lately." Heartsick, Kylie fought back waves of senseless emotion. The ring wasn't just a piece of jewelry. It was her protection, a symbol of who she'd been and who she was. But she couldn't expect Shane to understand that.

"Think. Where's the last place you remember having it?"

"I remember sitting at the table with Amy and Muriel. We were icing cookies—that's all I remember except that things got hectic after that, and I didn't miss the ring till now."

"Well, it's not going anywhere. Get a good night's rest and look in the morning. Maybe you'll remember then."

"What if I dropped it in the snow?"

"Then it'll be there when the snow melts."

"How can you be so . . . so . . ." *So, what? Callous? Unfeeling?* Kylie groped for the right word and failed to find it.

"You were saying?"

"Never mind." She exhaled, settling back in the seat. Shane wouldn't understand. He probably thought she was being a sentimental ninny. After all, a ring was only a piece of metal; he'd just helped her find the most precious thing of all— her son. But it wasn't the ring itself that mattered.

It was everything that simple gold band stood for. Now it was lost, and most likely for good.

A tear drizzled down her cheek, then another. Before she knew it, she was sobbing. It was not just for the ring, but for all the rest: losing Brad, losing their home, and failing to provide her children with the perfect lives they deserved. She couldn't even give them a decent Christmas. So many failures for the girl whom classmates at Branding Iron High School had voted "Most Likely to Succeed."

With a muted curse, Shane swung the truck onto the snow-piled shoulder of the road, shifted into neutral, and pulled the hand brake. Unfastening his seat belt, he turned and gathered her against his coat.

Resistance fading, Kylie nestled against him. He smelled of snow, fresh hay, and damp leather. His arms were even stronger than she'd imagined in her teenage dreams. "Go ahead and cry, girl," he murmured against her hair. "Heaven knows you've got your reasons. But things will come around in their own time. You'll see."

Kylie made a feeble effort to answer him, but her throat choked off the words. No one had put their arms around her since the day of Brad's funeral. The rare times she'd cried, she'd shed her tears alone, to spare her children. How could Shane have known this was what she needed? Until now, she hadn't even known it herself.

Driven by a hunger too deep to understand, she tilted her face upward. For the space of a breath, his hooded gaze held hers in the darkness of the cab. Then he lowered his head and captured her lips—not in a tender nibble like he'd given her the night before, but in a deep, sensual, soul-melting kiss.

Kylie's pulse slammed, pumping heat through her body. Buried hungers she'd tried to forget stirred and awakened like budding flowers. She found herself responding, arching upward to deepen that intoxicating kiss. Stars spun in her head. Comets trailed swirls of light.

Heaven help me, I want him.

Abruptly he pulled away. "Enough of that for now." His breathing was edgy, and his voice thick. "We've got a sleeping boy in the back and we need to get both of you home. Are you all right?"

"Yes. Let's get going." Feeling foolish now, Kylie settled into place. As Shane pulled back onto the road, she glanced over the seat at Hunter. Her son was sleeping like a tired puppy.

Would it have upset Hunter if he'd seen Shane kissing her? Maybe not. He liked Shane, maybe even had secret hopes that they might get together. But it wasn't going to happen. Delicious as that kiss had been, she'd be a fool to lose her heart to a man bent on wandering. Her long-distance marriage to Brad had been difficult

157

enough. If she ever settled on a man again, it would be someone who'd stay with her and be a full partner in raising their family—*not* "Love 'em and Leave 'em" Shane Taggart.

They drove the last mile in silence, with Shane keeping his eyes on the snow-slicked road. He couldn't help but wonder what Kylie was thinking. Best guess? She was already beating herself up for letting him kiss her—and for kissing him back. Shane Taggart, town bad boy and bad influence on young children.

But a pretty good kisser.
Damn!

For the second time, he'd broken his vow not to mess with a woman wearing a wedding ring. That she'd lost the ring, and was crying about it, was just a technicality. As far as Kylie was concerned, she was still married to a hero husband buried in Arlington. How could he measure up to that?

But what was he thinking? Why should he care if he measured up or not? If the prospective buyers closed on the ranch, he could be out of here in the next few weeks. Kylie and her little family would be history.

He exhaled, blowing off the tension as the lights of Muriel's place came into view around the bend. He and Kylie were already behaving as if that torrid kiss had never happened. When they got to the house, the charade would continue. But forgetting the hungry heat that had passed between them would be easier said than done. Lying in bed tonight, he'd be remembering every searing second of it. And something told him Kylie would be remembering, too.

By the time the truck pulled up to the house, Muriel, Henry, and Amy had come out onto the back porch. "Did you find him?" Amy called out as Kylie opened the door and jumped to the ground.

"He's right here in the back," Kylie said. "He's fine, just tired."

Shane had come around the truck to open the rear door of the cab. "Come on, sleepyhead, you're home."

Still groggy, Hunter sat up, blinking in the porch light. Shane untangled him from the quilt and boosted him to the ground.

"Where was he?" Amy asked.

"At a place called Buckaroo's," Shane said. "Our boy's had quite an adventure. I'll let him tell you about it."

The frigid air had shocked Hunter awake. "I hitched a ride with this old lady driving a pickup," he said. "She let me off at Buckaroo's. I thought maybe I could meet some new friends there. But there was nobody my age, just this really mean-looking gang of bikers."

Amy's eyes widened. "Were you scared?"

"Me? Heck, no. They were cool. Even gave me high fives."

"Wow!" Amy said.

"For heaven's sake, it's freezing out here!" Muriel pulled her woolen afghan tighter around her shoulders. "Come on inside. There's hot cocoa on the stove."

She ushered the children back inside. Henry followed, closing the door and leaving Kylie and Shane alone on the back porch.

Kylie looked up at him, ignoring the slight tremor that rippled all the way to her toes. The faint moonlight, reflecting on the snow, cast his eyes in shadow and highlighted the chiseled planes of his face. The urge to stretch on tiptoe and kiss those gorgeous lips again was almost too powerful to resist. But resist she did.

"Are you coming in?" she asked.

He shook his head. "It's getting late. I'll be heading home to a hot shower and a soft bed."

The mental image conjured by his words triggered a flush of heat to her face. Kylie tried the old trick of imagining an eraser wiping out the pictures in her head. It didn't work.

"I hope you know how grateful I am," she said. "Without you, I would never have known where to find Hunter."

"No need to thank me," he said. "Hunter's a good kid. I was concerned about him, too. I just hope he's learned a few lessons."

"Anyway . . ." She hesitated, expecting him to turn and go. Was he waiting for her to say something about the kiss, or even for some sign that he should kiss her again? "About what happened—"

"I know. It was nothing. A weak moment that's best forgotten."

The back door creaked open again. Muriel stood framed by light from the kitchen. "Are you two coming in? I've poured the cocoa, and it's getting cold."

"I was about to leave," Shane said.

"Nonsense, Cowboy. You've got time for a hot mug. It'll warm your belly for the drive home."

Still, he hesitated. "I'd—"

"Oh, come on in," Muriel said. "The mugs are on the table. I even squirted whipped cream on top."

"Can't say no to that." Shane surrendered, holding the door for Kylie as they followed Muriel into the kitchen, where the others were already seated. The chocolate was hot and sweet. The cream made white mustaches on the children's upper lips. Looking at each other across the table, they giggled.

"So I guess all's well that ends well," Muriel said.

"Not quite, I'm afraid." Kylie held up her left hand. "I've lost my ring. I hope you'll all keep your eyes open for it."

"Oh, dear," Muriel said. "Of course we will."

"Does that mean you're not married to Daddy anymore?" Amy asked.

An awkward silence hung over the table. Kylie felt Shane's eyes on her.

"All it means is that the ring's not on my finger," she said. "Maybe tomorrow you can help me look for it, Amy."

Henry emptied his mug and rose from his chair. "I'll be turning in," he said. "There's a good college game on TV. It should be starting about now. Thanks for the cocoa, Muriel. That was right nice of you." With a good-night nod to the others, he ambled out the back door.

Kylie glanced at her children. Amy looked tired. Hunter was yawning. "Time for bed, both of you," she said. "Don't forget to brush your teeth. Hunter, before you get ready for bed, I want a word with you—upstairs."

Hunter's expression told her he knew what was coming. He'd broken rules and would have to face the consequences. He rose from his seat and slunk toward the stairs.

"I'll be going, too," Shane said, rising. "Thanks for the cocoa, Muriel."

"Wait, Cowboy." Muriel's voice stopped him. "Stay a minute and talk with an old woman. I have something to get off my chest. Don't worry, it won't take long."

As Kylie left the kitchen and followed her son upstairs, Shane took his seat again. Muriel looked serious. What was on her mind?

He was about to find out.

Chapter Nine

"What's up, Muriel?" Shane studied his longtime neighbor across the table. He'd known Muriel Summerfield since his boyhood. They'd shared years of casual conversation, but this was the first time in memory she'd asked him to sit down for a serious talk. "Is something wrong?" he asked, suddenly concerned. "Are you all right?"

"Oh, I'm fine." She gave him a smile. "This isn't about me, Cowboy. It's about you."

"About *me?*" A prickle of apprehension crawled up Shane's backbone.

"About you and that lady who just left us."

Shane stifled a groan. He should've guessed what the woman was up to. "Whoa! Kylie and I are just friends, if that's what you're getting at." It was a bald-faced lie if he'd ever heard one. His relationship with Kylie could hardly be called "friendly." Throw in that kiss, and their connection was more like a lightning storm.

Muriel leaned closer across the table, her voice dropping to a conspiratorial whisper. "Listen, I'm getting too old to waste time beating around the bush. I know you're planning to sell and leave. But if you're looking for what's missing in your life, maybe you should stop and look around. Right here, you've got a woman, who lights you up like a Christmas tree, and two wonderful kids, who need a father. You've been lonesome all your life, Cowboy. If you hit the road on your bike, you'll go on being lonesome, maybe for the rest of your life. But it doesn't have to be that way. You could have it all. You could have a real family."

Shane shook his head. "You're jumping the gun, Muriel. Even if I agreed with you—and I'm not saying I do—the lady's still wearing her wedding ring—or, at least, she's searching for it. She's still married to her late husband. I can't compete with a dead war hero."

"Horsefeathers! I've noticed the way she looks at you. She may be fighting the attraction, but a little encouragement from you could win her over."

"What if I were to win her over, along with the kids, and then still decide to leave? Sorry, Muriel, I know you mean well. But when I hit the road, I want a clean getaway with no emotional baggage left behind."

Muriel's mouth formed a girlish pout. "Promise me you'll at least keep an open mind. All right?"

Shane stood. "I'm not in a position to promise anything. Helen's found a prospective buyer for the ranch, a couple from up north. They're coming to look at the place after the holidays. If they take it, I'll be out of here early."

Muriel sighed. "Well, at least that gives you a little time. Think it over, Cowboy. You may be riding away from your one chance at happiness."

He gave her a scowl. She only smiled. "Yes, I know I'm an old busybody, sticking my nose where it doesn't belong. But I think the world of Kylie and those young ones—and I think the world of you. To see all of you together as a family would give me a happy old age."

Lord, but this woman knows how to twist that guilt knife.

"Put it out of your mind, Muriel," he said. "I could give you a whole list of reasons why it wouldn't work. But it's getting late, so I'm going to leave before I start on them. Good night, and thanks again for the cocoa. Tell Henry I'll be back tomorrow to work on the bike."

With that, he headed out the back door.

Kylie returned to the kitchen to find Muriel alone at the table. "Where's Shane?" she asked. "I wanted to pass on Hunter's thanks for finding him."

"He just walked out," Muriel said. "You might be able to catch him. Either way, he'll be back tomorrow to work on the bike."

As Kylie hurried out onto the porch, she heard the slam of the truck door and the growl of the starting engine. An instant later, Shane's pickup rolled down the snowy drive toward the gate.

She paused, her spirits sinking. Foolish as the idea was, she'd looked forward to thanking him again and seeing him off. But she was too late. She'd missed him.

Not that it should matter. Muriel had said he was coming back. Hunter could thank him in person tomorrow.

Tomorrow!

Tomorrow was Christmas Eve. Christmas Eve with no tree and no presents. Nothing but the same old Christmas music on the radio and the lame Christmas reruns on TV.

Kylie watched the red taillights vanish down the road. She'd had such wonderful plans for this holiday. But they'd all gone as flat as punctured party balloons. She was running out of options. And she had no one to blame but herself.

December 24

The sky was pink with winter sunrise when the delivery van came rolling through the gate. Kylie and her children were sharing Muriel's favorite breakfast of hot oatmeal with cream and brown sugar. Through the kitchen window, Amy spotted the big brown vehicle. With a squeal, she jumped out of her chair and dashed for the front door. Kylie and Hunter rushed after her.

The three of them were standing on the front steps when the driver came up the shoveled walk, carrying a cardboard box large enough to hide his upper body from sight. Was it the Christmas presents or the warm winter clothes she'd ordered? Either one would be welcome, but she knew what her children were hoping for.

"Here you go. Merry Christmas." The driver set the box down on the porch. Kylie glanced at the label. It was from the online store where she'd ordered their coats, gloves, and boots—not the presents.

"I was expecting two boxes," she said. "Is there another one for us in your van?"

The driver shook his head. "Sorry. It's probably in a different shipment. But don't give up. We're doing our best to get everything delivered by Christmas."

As he hurried back to the van, Kylie turned to her downcast children. "Hey, don't look so sad! You have new, warm winter clothes! Amy, now you can play in the snow. Hunter, you don't have to wear that old plaid coat anymore. And our presents may still get here in time."

Amy managed a smile. "Let's go in and open the box. At least we'll be opening something."

"Good idea." Kylie reached for the box, but Hunter grabbed it, hoisted it to his shoulder, and carried it inside. Last night they'd discussed his punishment for running away and causing so much worry. Grounding him seemed useless, since he was already pretty much confined to the farm. But he'd lost his phone privileges for a week. To his credit, he hadn't argued or whined about it. Her son was growing up.

"Leave the box by the sofa, Hunter," she said. "We'll need to finish breakfast before we open it."

"Aw, Mom, it'll only take a minute."

"It'll keep. Finish your breakfast before it gets cold. After the table's cleared, we'll open the box."

The meal was finished and the table cleared in record time. Then Hunter and Amy tore into the box. The children had picked out their own winter clothes online, so there were no surprises. Still, they were excited to have something new. The puffy, hooded coats were quilted with synthetic down fill; Amy's was deep rose, Hunter's navy blue. The sturdy boots were lined with warm fleece. The gloves were wool.

Kylie's coat was emerald green, a color that flattered her fair hair and complexion. "Now I can stop borrowing your coat, Aunt Muriel," she said, pirouetting to show it off.

"It's lovely, dear." Muriel began running water on the breakfast dishes.

"No, you don't!" Kylie pulled off the coat and flew to the sink to nudge her aside. "You cooked breakfast. I'll do the dishes. Just sit down and keep me company."

"Well, if you insist." Muriel took a seat at the table as Hunter and Amy, already dressed in their warm winter outfits, dashed out the back door to play in the snow. Kylie added a squirt of detergent to the warm water and began washing the dishes.

"You haven't found your ring yet?" Muriel asked.

"No, and I've looked everywhere."

"So have I, dear. This morning before you came down to breakfast, I searched every inch of the kitchen. When I see Henry, I'll ask him to take the drain apart, in case it's fallen down there."

"I'm so sorry for the trouble," Kylie said. "My big worry is that I lost the ring outside in the snow."

"Well, dear, sooner or later, the snow will melt."

"That's just what Shane said."

Muriel sat in silence for a moment. A ray of morning light filtered through the window to gleam on her soft silver hair. "Did you ever stop to think that you might have lost your ring for a reason?" she asked.

Kylie turned to stare at her. "Whatever do you mean?"

"Somebody needs to say this, Kylie. You've been a widow for nineteen months, and your husband had been gone for nearly a year when you lost him. Maybe the disappearance of your ring is a sign."

"A sign?"

"A sign that it's time to move on."

Something tightened in Kylie's throat. Muriel was a wise woman, but she'd never married. What did she know about love and loss? "Move on? But what is there to move on to, Aunt Muriel?"

"You're still young and pretty, and you have so much to give. There's a new life waiting for you out there. All you need is to open yourself to it."

Kylie shook her head and went back to washing the dishes. How could she just walk away from her vows and memories? How could she let go of the past when, apart from her children, the past was all she had?

"What about you, Aunt Muriel?" she said, deliberately changing the subject. "When Amy asked you why you never married, you said the right man never asked you. So I'm wondering, *was* there a right man?"

"Perhaps." A little smile flickered across her lips. For a moment, she looked young.

"Who was he? What was his name?"

"His name doesn't matter anymore." Muriel's eyes seemed to be gazing into the past. "He worked for my father. I fell in love the first time I set eyes on him. But he was never anything but polite and respectful toward me. I suspect if he cared for me at all, he thought I was too fine for him. How wrong he was."

"So you never encouraged him?"

"I was shy, nothing like girls are these days. I had no idea how to encourage a man. And later on, of course, I had my father to take care of."

"So, what finally happened?"

"Nothing. We just got old." Still wearing that faraway look, Muriel got up and left the kitchen.

Deep in musings, Kylie finished the dishes. She'd told herself that her great-aunt knew nothing about love and loss. But she'd been wrong. No doubt Muriel had been talking about Henry, who'd stayed by her side all these years without ever speaking his mind. It was a beautiful love story—but such a sad one.

Was it too late for the two of them? Would they go to their graves without knowing the truth? Something needed to change. But how could she nudge them in the right direction without embarrassing two very dignified, very private people? Or even worse, wrecking a relationship built on years of trust?

She was drying the dishes when Amy burst into the kitchen. Her coat was dusted with snow. Her eyes were dancing. "Henry told us how to make snow angels! It's fun! Come out and play with us, Mom!"

Play?

For Kylie the word had almost lost its meaning. How long had it been since she'd put aside her worries and played with her children? How long since she'd laughed with them? In the months since Brad's death, every day had been about survival, with no time or energy for anything else. She'd missed playing, she realized. So had her children, especially Amy.

"Please, Mom." Amy tugged at her arm.

Giving in, Kylie tossed the dish towel aside and grabbed her new coat and boots. "I haven't made snow angels since I was your age," she said. "Let's see if I can remember how."

It was cold outside. Amy and Hunter's faces were flushed from playing in the snow. Their breaths made white puffs of vapor in the icy air. But it was their smiles Kylie noticed first. She couldn't remember when she'd seen her children look so happy.

"Come on, Mom!" Amy dashed into the knee-deep snow. "Let's see you make a snow angel!"

Kylie put up the hood of her coat and pulled her new gloves out of the pockets where she'd stuffed them.

"Right here." Amy guided her to a patch of fresh untouched snow. Kylie braced herself for the shock, took a deep breath and willed herself to fall straight backward. She gasped as the snow closed around her. The landing was like a tumble into icy cold feathers, but the lower layers of snow supported her weight and kept her from sinking too deep. Remembering what to do, she butterflied her arms up and down to make angel wings and thrashed her legs apart and together to make the skirt. Done. Now to get up without wrecking her angel.

"Help!" She held up her arms. Hunter and Amy each grabbed a hand and pulled. Kylie staggered to her feet, lost her balance and, laughing, fell back on her rear. Her perfect angel was ruined, but the sound of her children's laughter had been worth it.

"Make another one!" Amy said.

"Not on your life!" Kylie brushed the snow off her jeans. "I've got a better idea. Let me show you how to play Fox and Geese."

After morning chores and a quick breakfast, Shane drove his pickup over the snowy road to Muriel's farm. He'd planned on spending a few hours in the shed, examining the wrecked bike and judging which parts were usable. So far, Henry hadn't sounded optimistic about fixing it. But Shane wasn't ready to give up. When the ranch sold, he'd have plenty of money for a new top-of-the-line machine. But the idea of touring the back roads on his old Harley had the ring of a promise kept. He would do his best to keep the patient alive.

Kylie would be there, he reminded himself as he turned up the drive. But he planned to keep his distance. Kissing her last night had almost melted his boot soles. But he couldn't allow it to mean anything. He was almost a free man. Getting tangled up with a pretty widow and her two likable kids was the last thing he needed. And as far as he could tell, the lady felt the same way toward him.

Up ahead, between the barnyard and the house, something was going on. Dressed in jewel-colored coats, Kylie and her children were romping in the snow, falling down, getting up, and pelting each other with snowballs. Their winter clothes and boots must've arrived.

Shane's foot eased off on the gas as he neared the house. Rolling down the window, he could hear them shouting. The sight of Kylie, tumbling and playing in the snow like a little girl, made him want to sit back and enjoy watching her. Seeing her sparkle like that—her face flushed with cold, her mouth laughing—almost made him want to fall in love with her. But what was he thinking? Was Muriel's advice getting to him?

They'd noticed him now. Their play stopped as Shane pulled the truck up to the house and parked. Kylie waved at him as he climbed to the ground. "Hunter has something to tell you," she said, motioning her son over.

Hunter shuffled his new boots in the snow. "I'm sorry I ran away and caused so much trouble, Shane. Thanks for coming to drive me home."

Shane gave him a serious look. "Thanks for your apology, Hunter. I hope you've learned your lesson."

Hunter nodded sheepishly. "Are we square?"

"I'd say so." Shane allowed himself to smile. "When you're through playing in the snow, you're welcome to come out to the shed. Henry and I will be working on the bike. If you want to watch, maybe you can learn a thing or two."

"Hey, I'd like that!" Hunter chased off after his sister, who'd just thrown a snowball at his back. Kylie stood looking up at Shane, her eyes narrowed against the glare of sun on snow.

"Sorry if I overstepped myself," Shane said. "I guess I should've asked your permission before I invited him out to the shed."

"No, it's fine," she said. "It'll be something new for him—the sort of thing he'd never learn from his mother. It hasn't been easy, raising a boy on my own and trying to teach him man skills."

"So you aren't worried about my being a bad influence on him?" Shane couldn't resist needling her.

"Oh, stop it! I was just being overprotective. Given the way you came to our rescue last night, I feel like a fool."

"You're anything but a fool, Kylie. And I'd say you're doing a fine job of teaching your son man skills—like courtesy and responsibility."

Her laugh was brief but warm. "Sometimes I wonder about that. But thanks for the vote of confidence."

She'd made no move to leave. The eyes that

looked up at him were as blue as the favorite marble he'd carried in his pocket as a boy. Perfect little Kylie Summerfield. Was she thinking about last night's gasket-blowing kiss? He sure as hell was. And right now, he wouldn't mind a replay. Too bad they had an audience.

Something thumped against the back of Shane's coat. Turning around, he saw a grinning Amy about to fling a second snowball at him. He threw his hands in the air. "Hey, I surrender! Name it—anything you want!"

She lowered her hand. Her eyebrows slid together in a mock scowl. "You owe me a snowmobile ride," she said. "You took Hunter, but I didn't have a coat, so I couldn't go. Now I can go, and I want to see your puppies. Hunter says you have horses, too." She caught her mother's frown. "Please," she added.

Shane took a moment to weigh her demand. "Tell you what," he said. "I'll take you, but only if your mom will come along, too. With you on her lap, you should both fit on the rear seat."

Amy was dancing up and down. "Can we go right now? Please say yes, Mom!"

"Is now all right?" Kylie asked. "I know you were planning to work on your bike, but I hate to disappoint her."

"No problem. Now's as good a time as any. Hang on and I'll get the snowmobile out of the shed."

Shane was turning to go when Henry stepped out onto the back porch, carrying a heavy pipe wrench. "Sorry, Kylie," he said. "I took the kitchen drain apart and looked in the trap. When your ring wasn't there, I checked the bathroom drains, too. No sign of it."

Kylie sighed. "Thanks for trying, Henry. That ring's got to be somewhere. I won't stop searching till it's back on my finger."

Seeing her dejected look, Shane turned away and strode off to get the snowmobile. Muriel had put up a good argument for getting serious about Kylie. But she'd been wrong about one thing: Kylie's heart was buried in Arlington with her husband—and that wasn't likely to change.

Kylie clasped her daughter close as the snowmobile roared toward the Taggart ranch. Seated in front of them, Shane's broad shoulders blocked the view ahead. He'd cut away from the road to zip across the open field, and Amy was loving it. She squealed with laughter as the flying snow spattered her face. It had been a long time since Kylie had seen her little girl so happy. And it was mostly Shane's doing. The man would make a wonderful father—if any woman could get him to stay put.

They were nearing the heart of the ranch. Kylie remembered the place from her growing-up years. She'd always admired the house, with its broad front porch and Craftsman-style architecture. Shane's father had built it for his wife. But after her illness and death from cancer, he'd stopped caring about the place and it had fallen into neglect. Kylie had dropped Shane off here two days ago, after wrecking his bike. But it had been storming then; the air had been filled with flying snow. Only now, as she saw the house in full daylight, did she appreciate how much Shane had done to restore its faded beauty.

"I always did love your house," she said as he switched off the noisy engine. "I can tell you've done a lot of work on it. It seems a shame to put it up for sale."

"I've had the same thought," he said. "But this house deserves to be a happy place with a family inside. It hasn't been a happy place for a long time."

"I want to see the puppies!" Amy said.

"They're in the barn. Come on, I'll show you." Shane helped her off the snowmobile. She raced ahead down the shoveled path, with Shane and Kylie following.

"She's quite a girl," Shane said. "Reminds me a lot of you at that age."

Kylie laughed. It felt good, that laughter coming out of a place that had been silent too long. "She looks a lot like I did. But I was far too serious back then. So far, Amy's favorite thing seems to be having fun."

"You're still too serious," Shane said. "You try too hard and then you beat yourself up because life isn't perfect. You can't accept the fact that it's just life."

"Since when did you get so smart? Is giving my children a decent Christmas asking too much —especially when, so far, what they're getting is no Christmas at all?" Kylie kicked at a chunk of snow on the path. "I can't just give up. I've got to think of a way to make things all right."

At that moment, an idea sprang to her mind— not a great idea, but better than none at all. She would keep it to herself for now.

"Come on!" Amy had reached the barn door.

"Hold your horses!" Catching up with her, Shane unfastened the latch and opened the door partway. Light shone through the high windows below the roof. "Calm and quiet, Amy," he said. "No running or squealing. That's the way to behave around animals."

"Got it." She halted her wild dash into the barn and proceeded on tiptoe. Kylie caught the flicker of a smile on Shane's lips. She stayed back, watching him with her daughter.

"Oh . . . horses!" Amy spoke in an excited whisper. "Can I pet one?"

"Sure. Hang on." Shane moved a sturdy wooden crate in front of the nearest stall. The bay mare, expecting attention, put a nose over the high gate. Amy, who'd never been so close to a horse, looked hesitant. As if stalling, she pulled off her gloves and stuffed them in her pockets.

"Climb up and get acquainted," Shane said. "Don't be scared. She won't hurt you."

"She's so big. Is she really a girl?"

"A very nice girl. Her name's Daisy."

"Hi, Daisy." Still a little uncertain, Amy climbed onto the crate and put up her hand. The mare sniffed her palm. Amy giggled. "She tickles!"

"Try this." Stepping closer, Shane took her wrist and guided her hand to the mare's smooth cheek. "Pet her here. She likes that."

"Wow!" Amy's eyes widened. "She feels like silk. Can I ride her when the snow's gone?"

"Maybe—if I'm still here by then."

"You're *going?*" The horse forgotten, Amy turned to him with a shattered look.

"My ranch is for sale," Shane said. "As soon as somebody buys it, I'll be leaving to travel the country on my motorcycle."

Amy looked ready to cry. "But you can't leave! We need you!"

It was time for Kylie to step in. "Sometimes people leave, Amy. They leave because they want to, or because they have to. That's just how life is. We'll miss Shane when he goes, but we'll be fine."

Tears welled in Amy's blue eyes. "But when my dad left, he never came home!"

In the silence that followed, Kylie's gaze met

Shane's. She shook her head. There were no words.

"Hey, I think it's time to meet the puppies," Shane said, boosting her down from the box. "They're in that first stall with their mom. Come on!"

Brightening, Amy scampered after him.

The puppies were tumbling in their spacious box. One of the little females had been taken home that morning by her new family. Of the three that were left, two would be gone before the holidays were over, leaving only little Mickey and his mother.

"Oh!" Amy dropped to her knees beside the box. "They're so cute! Can't I have one, Mom? Please? Aunt Muriel said a dog would be all right."

"You know what Hunter told us," Kylie reminded her daughter. "These pups are all spoken for."

"That's right," Shane said. "A rancher friend of mine has bought both these little girls. And I'm keeping the boy for myself. His name's Mickey."

Mickey had made a beeline for Amy. When she scooped him up in her arms, he wagged his tail and licked her face. "Oh, he's the cutest one of all!" she crooned.

"He's a special dog," Shane said. "His father used to ride on the motorcycle with me. He died this past fall. Mickey's his very last son."

"Is Mickey going to ride on your motorcycle, too?"

"That's the plan," Shane said.

"But he's too little." Amy's eyes would have melted a heart of granite.

"He'll grow. And I can already tell he's smart enough to learn."

"What if he falls off and gets hurt?"

"I can fix a special place on the bike so that won't happen."

Kylie reached past them to pet the mother dog. "She's beautiful. What are your plans for her? Will she have more pups?"

"These are her last," Shane said. "After I make sure of that, she's going to a boy who's worked for me the past few summers. Her name's Sheila, by the way."

"Hi, Sheila." Still holding the pup, Amy scratched the dog's silky ears with her free hand. "I love your babies."

"It sounds like you've got everything figured out," Kylie said. "What about the horses?"

"They're great cow ponies. They'll stay here if the new owner wants them. If not, I'll sell them to other ranchers or even give them away to good homes."

"Mom!" Amy tugged at Kylie's coat. "We could take Daisy! Hunter and I could learn to ride her!"

Kylie sighed. "That's enough, Amy. Nobody's giving us a horse."

Shane glanced at his watch. "What do you say we get back? Henry will be waiting to help me with the bike."

"Okay. As soon as I kiss Mickey good-bye." Amy planted a smack on the pup's dark head and put him down by his mother.

They returned the easier way, by the road. Kylie kept a secure grip on her daughter, but her thoughts were on the tall, dark-haired man driving the snowmobile. Shane's talk about leaving wasn't just talk. He was making solid plans to go. She'd tried to tell herself she didn't care, but she knew better.

The truth was, more and more, she found herself wanting the long, tall Texan to stay.

By the time the snowmobile pulled up to the house, they'd been gone more than an hour. Shane switched off the engine and helped his passengers off the machine.

"Thanks for the ride, Shane," Amy said. "It was neat."

"Yes, thank you." Kylie tried to catch his eye with a smile, but he seemed preoccupied. He held the back door open for her and Amy; then he followed them inside, where Muriel was just taking a sheet of oatmeal raisin cookies out of the oven. The spicy, fresh-baked aroma filled the kitchen.

Muriel set the cookie sheet on the counter. "As soon as they're cool, you can help yourselves.

But while we're waiting, I have a surprise for you. Close your eyes, Amy. No peeking till I say so."

Moving behind Amy, Muriel put her hands on the girl's shoulders and guided her toward the parlor. Looking past them, Kylie could see the waiting surprise. Her heart sank. Standing in a corner of the room was Muriel's old flocked-foil Christmas tree, decorated with tinsel, lights, and the precious ornaments they'd brought from California. Dear Muriel had acted with the kindest of intentions. But the tree . . . Kylie shuddered.

"Open your eyes, Amy," Muriel said. "Surprise!"

Amy opened her eyes, took one look at the silver tree, and burst into tears.

Chapter Ten

Shane opened the door to the machine shed and stepped inside. Warmed by a small electric space heater, the air was chilly but tolerable. He slid the door closed behind him. Pulling off his sheepskin coat, he laid it over a handy sawhorse.

Henry and Hunter were inspecting the scattered motorcycle parts. The old man was sitting on a low wooden stool; the boy was kneeling on the cement floor. They both looked up as Shane walked toward them.

"So, what did my sister do when she saw Aunt Muriel's tree?" Hunter asked.

"I'm afraid she cried."

"I told Aunt Muriel that Amy wouldn't like it. But she said it'd be better than no tree at all. When she asked me to get the box out of the attic and help set it up, I did what she wanted. But I knew what was going to happen and I didn't want to stick around. Amy can be such a baby when she doesn't get her own way."

"Was Muriel upset?" Henry asked. "She's such a gentle soul. I hope her feelings weren't hurt."

"Muriel took it like the lady she is." Shane frowned at the array of bike pieces. "So, what do you think, Henry? Can we fix it?"

"Dunno." Henry shook his head. "There are some pretty mangled parts here. If we can't weld them back into shape, we'll need to find replacements. And for a bike this old . . ."

Shane understood what he'd left unsaid. The chances weren't good. "Well, we can at least try. What do you say we start with a triage—usable parts, fixable parts, and parts that'll need replacing. You can help us sort them, Hunter."

The boy's face lit up. "You said something about welding. Could I learn to do that?"

This wasn't Shane's call to make. He glanced at Henry.

"I could show you a few things," the old man said. "But welding can be dangerous work. You'd need to clear it with your mother."

Hunter scowled. "Not much chance of that. Not with my mom. She treats me like I'm the same age as Amy."

Just then, the shed door slid partway open. As if conjured by the mention of her name, Amy slipped inside. Her new pink coat was unzipped; her face was streaked with salty-tear lines.

"Close the door," Hunter said. "Is Mom mad at you?"

"A little bit." Amy pulled the door shut behind her. "I told Aunt Muriel I was sorry. I didn't mean to make her feel bad. She was only trying to do something nice. But I was wishing so hard for us to have a real Christmas tree. And all we got was an ugly old silver one that doesn't have a smell. It doesn't even have any presents under it."

"So, what did you come out here for?" Hunter asked.

"I came to watch. Mom said it was okay. I think she needed a break."

Shane found her a box to sit on. "You can watch from here, Amy," he said. "If you have any good ideas or any questions, just speak up."

"Okay." Amy managed a smile.

"Was your Aunt Muriel all right, Amy?" Henry asked her. "You said she felt bad."

"She did," Amy said. "But I think she felt better

after I said I was sorry. She hugged me and said it was fine."

Amy sat in silence for a few minutes, watching while Hunter and the two men sorted the broken, scattered motorcycle parts.

"What's this?" Hunter picked up a short, sturdy metal rod with fastenings at each end.

"That's the front-wheel axle," Shane said. "We're lucky it wasn't bent. It anchors the center of the wheel and lets it turn. Put it over there with the parts that are still good."

Amy had begun to squirm. At last, as if she couldn't hold the words back any longer, she spoke. "I have a good idea."

"Great. Tell us what it is," Shane said.

"I think Henry and Aunt Muriel should get married."

The crushed headlamp Henry was holding clattered to the cement. His face went beet red. "What in blazes put that cockeyed notion into your head?" he muttered.

"I know you and Aunt Muriel like each other," Amy said. "You're always taking care of each other. And you must be about the same age, so that part would be okay. If you got married, you could live in the house and not in that old trailer. So, what do you say?"

"I say your brain's full of soap bubbles, girl. A fine lady like your aunt Muriel would never want to marry a grubby old wrench jockey like me."

"Have you ever asked her?"

"No, and I don't plan to. So put that idea out of your silly head."

The old man was clearly uncomfortable. Shane broke in to change the subject. "So, what do you think of this mechanical mess now that we're into it, Henry?"

Henry exhaled, welcoming the rescue. "You know I'm happy to help you, Shane. And I know how much this old motorcycle means to you. But you need to think about what you'll do if it's busted for good."

"Guess I could always buy a new bike," Shane said. "But it wouldn't be the same. That's why I want to fix this one if there's any way."

"I hear you," Henry said. "And I know you've got plans. But just because you've always wanted to go gallivantin' around the country doesn't mean it's a good idea. Ever think about that?"

Startled by the question, Shane gazed down at the scattered parts—the crushed windscreen, the broken gauges, the nuts, bolts, and wires that were vital to the bike's operation. "Nothing more to think about. I've waited half my lifetime for this break. It's something I've dreamed of doing since I was in high school. If I hadn't needed to take care of the ranch and my father, I'd be long gone by now."

Henry tossed a mangled side mirror onto the replace pile. "Shane, I reckon you're the closest thing to a son I ever had. But you're not in high school anymore. You're thirty-three years old. The country's changed a lot since you first read Jack Kerouac and got it into your young fool head to hit the road. It's crowded and dirty and mean out there, and most of the people you meet won't give a damn about you."

"I read and I watch the news." Shane rose to his own defense. "It's not like I don't know what's going on in the world. And it's not like I can't handle bad situations. I've been doing that since I was a kid."

Shane glanced down at Hunter. The boy was wide-eyed, taking it all in. What was he learning from this conversation? And what about Amy, sitting on her box like a quiet little cat? Kylie's children wanted him to stay—that much he already knew. So did Henry, and so would Muriel.

But what about Kylie?

Kylie had never argued against his leaving. She'd accepted the idea as if it didn't matter. *"Sometimes people leave."* That was what she'd told her daughter. If she cared—cared about him—would he be more inclined to stay? But why bother to ask that question when Kylie was still searching for her ring and mourning her war hero husband?

"I don't doubt you can handle yourself," Henry said. "You've been punching bullies since you were in kindergarten. But look ahead, to the end of the road. Where will you go when you've seen it all? What will you do when you're burned out and getting old—when you can't come home because you sold your land, spent all the money, and cut your ties to the people who used to need you? I've seen men like that, Shane. So have you. I hate to think of you ending up one of them."

"That's a low blow, Henry." Shane tossed a broken gear mount onto the replace pile, which was growing faster and higher than the others.

"Maybe so." Henry's eyes narrowed. "But whatever it is you're looking for, I can almost guarantee you're not going to find it on the road. All that really matters is what's right here."

Shane countered with a question of his own. "You stayed when you could've left, Henry. If you'd gone someplace else, you could've traveled, had your own business, a nice home, a wife, and a family. But you chose to stay right here and work as a hired man on this farm. Don't you have any regrets?"

A faraway smile lit Henry's pale eyes. "No," he said. "Not a single one."

From the house, the brief hush that followed Henry's answer was broken by the jangle of the bell that hung outside the back door.

"Lunch!" Hunter scrambled to his feet. "I hope it's Mom's pizza! I'm starved!" He raced out the door, sprinting ahead of Shane and Henry, who took their coats and followed him. They were halfway to the house when Shane noticed Amy wasn't with them.

"Amy?" He paused, glancing around. "Amy, are you coming?"

When she didn't answer, he started back. Kylie wouldn't want her daughter left alone in a place with as many potential dangers as the machine shed.

He'd taken a few steps back toward the shed when she popped out the door. Her face wore an odd little grin. "Are you okay?" he asked.

"Sure. Just slow. I'm coming." Sliding the door shut, she skipped toward him, bouncing along the shoveled path. "Let's get some lunch!"

As Shane washed up in the half bath off the kitchen, the smell of homemade pizza made his mouth water. He couldn't recall ever having eaten pizza that didn't come across a counter or out of a delivery car.

Kylie was wearing one of Muriel's old-fashioned calico aprons over her jeans and sweater. She'd taken the pizzas out of the oven and was cutting them into slices. Her blond hair curled softly over cheeks that were flushed from the heat. He remembered how she'd looked that morning, romping in the snow with her children, her face glowing, her laughter sweet on the winter air. He'd always thought she was the prettiest girl in his class. Now she'd matured into a stunningly beautiful woman.

Looking past the kitchen into the parlor, he could see the silver-foil Christmas tree, the kind that had been popular back in the 1950s and '60s. In its day, the tree might have been called elegant. Looking at it now, hung with traditional-looking ceramic ornaments, Shane could sympathize with Amy's tears. The tree was a sorry substitute for the real thing. But at least Muriel had made the effort.

Shane remembered his own family Christmases, the ones before his mother's illness. The branches of the big, fresh pine tree, so tall it would barely fit beneath the ceiling, would be sagging with a glory of lights and ornaments. After her death, his father had boxed everything and taken it up to the attic, never to see another holiday.

Shane had not celebrated Christmas since.

The table was set for six with glasses of milk and a fresh green salad in a red enameled bowl. "Sit down, everybody," Kylie said, sliding the pizzas onto a tray. "Would you believe I'm finally figuring out how not to burn things in Muriel's oven?"

They joined hands for grace. Shane cradled Kylie's warm fingers in his palm as Muriel said a prayer, which ended all too soon. Where, on the road to adventure, would he find the spirit of friendship and family that lingered around this simple table? He imagined the solitary meals that, in time, would all taste the same. He thought of the nights in strange beds—some of them, perhaps, with strange women.

Was Henry's fatherly lecture getting to him?

No, he wasn't going to let that happen.

True, he wasn't a kid anymore. And America might not be as safe and friendly as in the old days. However, he'd treasured this dream too long to give it up. After all these years, how could he just toss it aside like an outgrown pair of shoes? As for Henry's argument about the future, he knew he wouldn't want to roam forever. He was bound to end up somewhere. It just wouldn't be here, where he'd felt trapped most of his life.

As they started on salad and pizza, Amy's piping voice broke into Shane's musings. "So, what are we going to do tonight?"

"What do you usually do on Christmas Eve?" Muriel asked.

"We sit around the tree and take turns reading the Christmas story from the Bible," Amy said. "Then we sing Christmas songs, have treats, and hang up our stockings. Finally we each get to open one present, which Mom picks out. Usually, it's pajamas. We put them on and go to bed."

"That sounds like a lovely Christmas Eve," Muriel said. "We could do that here."

"But we won't have anything to open," Amy said. "The brown truck hasn't come back, and I'm too old to believe Santa's on his way."

"When our dad was home, he used to play the guitar for us to sing," Hunter said. "He was a good singer. His songs sounded almost as good as the ones on the radio."

"I play the guitar." Shane could've kicked himself for volunteering that bit of information. "I taught myself, so I'm not very good. And I'm no singer. But if you want me . . ." His words trailed off. What had he been thinking? After Hunter's description of his father's talents, his own lame strumming of the half-dozen chords he knew would be an embarrassment.

"Thanks, Shane. That would be great." Kylie sounded almost too cheerful. "Singing always sounds better with someone playing along."

"Don't thank me till you've heard me." Shane reached for a slice of pizza, wishing he'd kept his mouth shut. He could've spent the evening at home enjoying a beer and a good crime novel, just like last year. Instead, he'd just invited himself to a celebration that could turn out to be an emotional train wreck.

The pizza was disappearing fast. Hunter was reaching for the last slice when Muriel spoke.

"We don't need everything perfect to have a good Christmas. We don't even need presents. That's not what the holiday's about."

"I know it's about Jesus' birthday," Hunter said. "But presents make it a lot more fun."

"Presents and a real Christmas tree." Amy caught herself. "Sorry, Aunt Muriel. I know you did your best."

"I remember the first Christmas after my father got this farm," Muriel said. "We couldn't go for a tree because it was snowing, so we decorated a big tumbleweed with paper chains. That was the year my only present was a pair of warm socks my mother had knitted. But it was a happy time. We were together as a family in our new home, on land that was—"

"Look!" Amy shouted, jumping up, toppling her chair in her excitement. "Look out the window! The delivery van's coming down the road!"

Without taking time to excuse themselves from lunch or put on their coats, the children raced for the front door, with Kylie on their heels. After an instant's hesitation, Shane rose and followed them out onto the front porch. Looking up the main road, he could see the brown van approaching the gate. But something wasn't as it should be. The van wasn't even slowing down.

"No!" Amy wailed, waving her arms as the big vehicle rolled past without stopping. "Come back here! Come back with our Christmas presents!"

"That driver doesn't have our presents, Amy." Kylie looked as devastated as her children. "If he'd had them, he'd have stopped here. Unless there's another delivery today, I'm afraid we're out of luck."

Shane surveyed the three gloomy faces. He knew how much it meant to Kylie to give her children a good Christmas. Given more time, she might have bought a few gifts elsewhere. But the nearest town big enough to have a shopping mall was sixty miles away, on icy roads. Here in Branding Iron, there was only Shop Mart, which carried groceries, home goods, and a few items like coloring books and crayons, cheap T-shirts, baseball caps, and socks—not the sort of gifts that would light up young eyes on Christmas morning.

A tear trailed down Amy's cheek. Hunter and Kylie looked like mourners at a funeral. There had to be something he could do to cheer them up.

"Hey, have you ever built a snow fort?" Shane seized on the first idea that sprang to mind.

Hunter shook his head. Amy blinked away a tear. "I'd rather make a snowman," she said.

"We can do that, too," Shane said. "Maybe your mom would like to help us."

Kylie hesitated. "I really need to—"

"Oh, please, Mom!" Amy tugged at her hand. "It'll be more fun with you helping."

Kylie's eyes met Shane's in a flickering glance. Was it gratitude he saw in her look or plain resignation? "Sure," she said. "But first you need to finish your lunch and help clean up. All right?"

"You bet!" Amy dashed back into the house. Hunter followed at a slower pace, leaving Shane and Kylie alone on the porch.

"Thanks." She sounded frayed. Tired shadows framed her eyes. "I appreciate the distraction."

"You don't have to join us if you need a break," he said. "I'm sure you've built a few snow forts in your day."

"I have, but not with my children. I'll see you out back in fifteen minutes."

Shane watched her walk back inside, wondering how much sleep she'd gotten the past few nights. Too bad he couldn't erase the worried shadows that framed her baby blue eyes. If he knew how and had the means, he would wrap up the perfect Christmas in a big red box, tie it with a ribbon, and leave it under that sad little Christmas tree. He could afford anything within reason, but the problem wasn't money. It was circumstances he had no power to change.

The snowman was no work of art. Its head sat on its body at a cockeyed angle, and one broomstick arm was longer than the other. Its eyes were unmatched buttons, its drawn-on smile was lopsided, and the carrot Muriel had donated from the root cellar didn't look much like a nose. But that didn't matter because Amy had had a wonderful time building it.

Kylie stood back and watched as Shane helped her daughter add an old scarf and hat to their creation. Behind them, in the unshoveled part of the yard, Hunter had already started rolling snowballs for the fort they were going to build.

Shane had done wonders for the children's spirits, laughing and joking with them as they played in the snow. After the disappointment of the missing Christmas package, it was the best gift he could have given the three of them.

She'd made a mistake, misjudging him at first. The bad boy she'd crushed on in high school had grown up to be a genuinely good man, responsible and giving. But that restless spirit still burned in him. Any woman who gave him her heart would be fated to have it shattered. And even if she could risk her own hurt, she couldn't risk hurting her children.

"Come on, Mom! Help us with the fort!" Hunter called. Kylie started across the yard. She'd made plans for the afternoon, but they could wait. Right now, the important thing was being here for her family.

Plunging through the snow, she stubbed her boot on a buried rock and pitched forward onto her face. Unhurt, she tried to push herself up, but the knee-deep snow offered no purchase for her hands. She floundered like a fish in shallow water, probably looking ridiculous. As the silliness of it struck, laughter bubbled up in her throat. By the time Shane reached her, she was giggling like a fifteen-year-old.

"I've got you." He caught her gloved hands and dragged her partway to her feet, but his own footing was unsteady. As he pulled her up, still laughing, she lost her balance and pushed him backward. He staggered and fell faceup in the soft snow. Kylie landed on top of him, her face a hand's breadth from his.

Suddenly she wasn't laughing anymore.

His dark eyes burned into hers. She saw the hunger in their depths and felt her own responding need. She was aware of his breathing and the solid, manly contact of his body against hers. The urge to lean down and kiss his firm mouth was tempered only by the awareness that her children were watching. For a fleeting moment, she forgot to breathe.

"Dog pile!" Hunter shouted, flinging himself crosswise over her back.

"Dog pile!" Amy shrilled, jumping aboard and triggering a free-for-all of flying snow, thrashing arms and legs, snow pummeling, and laughter that left them sprawled on their backs in the snow, out of breath.

Still giddy, Kylie sat up and brushed the snow out of her hair. "I don't remember the last time I laughed so hard," she said.

"Maybe when we were in tenth grade and somebody put a cockroach in Mr. Pratt's desk drawer?" Shane sat up, grinning.

"That somebody was you, Shane Taggart. I was walking by the classroom door after school and saw you do it."

"And you didn't tattle on me? Hey, even after all this time, I owe you one!" Shane rose to his knees and powered himself to his feet.

"Don't remind me," Kylie said. "I might decide to collect."

"That could turn out to be fun. Come on." He held out his hands. Gripped by their strength, she let him pull her up. They stood face-to-face, both of them coated with snow. Hunter and Amy were sitting up, watching. Kylie felt the rise of a long-buried memory—a memory that struck her with enough force to rock her world.

It was the dog pile game—a family game the children hadn't played since they were much younger, back when Brad was spending more time at home. On lazy weekend mornings, Hunter and Amy would sneak into the bedroom and leap onto the bed yelling, "Dog pile! Dog pile!" It was a rude awakening, but the laughing tussle that followed left everybody in a happy mood.

Until now, she'd forgotten all about that time. But it seemed her children hadn't—especially Hunter. Had today's laughing attack been all in fun, or were they trying to send her some kind of message? Confused and shaken, Kylie brushed the snow off her coat.

"So, is anybody still up for building a snow fort?" Shane asked.

"I'm freezing," Amy said. "I need to go in the house and get warm."

Kylie had begun to shiver. "I'm cold, too," she said. "And I have things to do before Christmas Eve. So if you don't mind excusing me . . ."

"How about you, Hunter?" Shane slid off his gloves and whacked them against his coat to knock off the snow. "Would you rather build a snow fort or go back to the shed and sort bike parts? Your call."

"It's getting cold out here," Hunter said. "I like learning about the bike. Let's try the shed."

"Guess that settles it. We can always finish the snow fort later. Let's go."

Kylie watched them walk away—her son stretching his legs to match Shane's stride. Her children had cast their votes, making it clear in their own way that they wanted Shane in their lives. Her own heart was pulling her in the same direction. But her practical, protective head was shouting, *No, no, no!*

She'd be a fool not to listen. Shane had made up his mind to leave. If she tried to stop him, he would only resent her for it.

Back in the house, she dried off, warmed up, and settled Amy in front of the TV soap operas, alongside Muriel, with a plate of oatmeal cookies and a glass of milk. Muriel had offered to show the girl how to crochet. Amy actually seemed interested in learning. At least it might keep her entertained for an hour or two.

Shabby and forlorn, the silver Christmas tree

stood in one corner of the room. Several of the branches had been crushed and bent. Most of the fake needles had lost their glittery "snow" flocking. The traditional ceramic ornaments Kylie had collected with so much love looked sadly out of place.

Kylie slipped on her coat. Somewhere out there, within driving distance, there had to be a real, green Christmas tree she could bring home to her children. Whatever it took, she vowed, she was not coming home without one.

Grabbing her purse, and whispering to Muriel that she had an errand to run, she went outside to the open vehicle shed, where she'd parked her station wagon. Shane had warned her about her slick tires, but by now the plowed road had seen plenty of traffic between here and town. If she drove carefully, she should be fine.

The plan she had in mind was a desperate one. Schools and businesses that closed for the holidays often threw their trees out before shutting down on Christmas Eve. If she drove the back alleys, checking Dumpsters and trash piles, she'd have a fair chance of finding a fresh enough tree to tie on top of the car and bring home.

Earlier that day, she'd found a ball of stout twine in the kitchen and put it in the backseat, along with a pair of scissors for cutting it. Those items would be enough to carry out Plan A. But for the even more desperate Plan B, she would need something extra.

Shane, Hunter, and Henry were in the machine shed where the tools were kept. But Shane's truck was parked nearby. Kylie had noticed the toolbox under the backseat, with the padlock hanging open from the hasp. Glancing around to make sure no one was watching, she opened the door and slid the box out from under the seat. With a bit of stealthy rummaging, she found what she needed—a small folding saw.

Whatever it took, she reminded herself as she started her car and backed into the yard. Whatever it took, she would come home with a real Christmas tree for her children.

<u>Chapter Eleven</u>

Henry surveyed the piles of sorted bike parts and shook his head. "I know how much you want your bike back the way it was, Shane. But from the looks of this mess, I'd say your only chance of ever riding it again would be to go on the Internet and look for the same model. If by chance you found one, especially one with a bad motor or smashed rear end that you could buy for a song and use for parts, we'd be in business. Otherwise"—Henry shrugged—"you might as well start shopping for a new one."

Shane had known the news was coming. But the bike was like an old friend. He couldn't just walk away and abandon it. "Thanks, but I'm not ready to give up," he said. "This is an old bike and a rare one. But when I go home tonight, I'll go online and start my search. Who knows? Maybe I'll get lucky and find something that'll work. Meanwhile, at least I can box up these parts and haul them out of your way. The bike might as well go, too."

"It's fine if you leave them here," Henry said. "There's plenty of room. We'll just stick everything in a corner till you've figured out what you want to do with it."

"Thanks. With the ranch up for sale and a possible buyer coming in a couple of weeks, nothing's settled right now."

Hunter had sat in silence, listening to the conversation. Now he spoke up. "Can I ask a favor? It's been cool helping you guys and learning about the bike parts. Can we leave them out here for a while so I can spend more time with them? Maybe one of you can even teach me a few things. I promise to put everything away when we're done."

"Fine with me," Shane said. "How about you, Henry?" Motorcycle mechanic probably wasn't the career Kylie had in mind for her son. But if the boy was interested, at least it would give him something to do.

"Sure," Henry said. "What do you say I show you something now, while we're here? Maybe . . ." He glanced around, then picked up the bent front wheel. "Maybe like the way this wheel is mounted."

"Cool." Hunter leaned forward, eyes bright with interest. "I remember picking up the axle and putting it . . ." He reached toward the pile of undamaged parts, then paused, frowning. "That axle was right here before lunch. Did anybody move it?"

"Not that I know of," Shane said. "And I saw you put it on that pile."

"Well, it isn't there now," Hunter said.

"Maybe we've got a pack rat holed up somewhere in the shed," Henry said.

"It'd have to be one husky pack rat to steal that axle," Shane said, keeping his own suspicions to himself. "What we've got here's an honest-to-goodness mystery."

"Hey, I like mysteries," Hunter said. "What d'you say we try to solve it? If the axle was here before lunch, where could it have gone? It didn't just sprout legs and walk off."

"Beats me." Shane's response was a half-truth. He had a pretty good idea what had happened but he was enjoying the boy's eagerness to play detective. "Maybe if we can find it, we'll know what happened."

They started with the piles of sorted bike parts

and went from there to the counters and cabinets. Shane even lifted up the box Amy had been sitting on, but there was no sign of the missing axle. Maybe his hunch had been wrong.

"Never mind, Hunter," Henry said with a shrug. "I reckon it'll turn up sooner or later. Let me show you something else."

"I'll leave you to it," Shane said. "It's time I was getting home. I need to tend the animals and get my guitar for tonight. I'll stop by the house and see what time the ladies want me to come."

He walked back across the yard, wishing he hadn't offered to play the guitar for Christmas Eve. He wasn't very good, and Kylie's children would doubtless compare his playing to their father's. But he'd do his best. Once he was on the road, with Branding Iron in his rearview mirror, it wouldn't make much difference.

As he passed the open vehicle shed, he noticed Kylie's car was gone. She'd probably made a last-minute run to town. Stubborn woman, he'd told her those old, bald tires were bad, but he should've known she wouldn't listen. He could only hope she'd be all right on the roads.

Coming in through the back door, he could hear the TV from the living room, where Muriel and Amy were probably watching a show. Amy's new pink coat hung on the back of a kitchen chair. Acting on a sudden hunch, Shane picked up the coat, held it upside-down and gave it a gentle shake.

Something solid and heavy dropped out of a pocket and hit the floor with a metallic clunk. Shane picked up the missing axle and waited. A moment later Amy walked into the kitchen, looking shamefaced.

"Why did you take this, Amy?" Shane asked.

She hesitated, fingers twisting the hem of her shirt. "I took it because I don't want you to fix the bike and leave," she said. "Think how selfish it would be—to go when so many people need you—Muriel and Henry, Mom and Hunter and me. Even your poor animals and that little pup who might not want to ride on your motor-cycle. How can you just ride away and not care?"

Shane felt as if he'd been stabbed through the heart. But he couldn't tell Amy what she wanted to hear. This was no time for anything but the truth. "I do care, Amy," he said. "But this road trip is something I've dreamed of for years. If I stay, I'll have to give up that dream, maybe forever."

"Then you don't care. Not enough. Go on. Keep your stupid dream. Maybe after a while we'll forget all about you."

Head high, she stalked out of the kitchen, leaving Shane with the axle in his hand and an unaccustomed tightness in his throat.

The snowpacked road was even more treacherous than Kylie had imagined. Crawling along in low gear at twenty miles an hour, she could feel her tires spinning on the icy surface. Her hands gripped the steering wheel so tightly that her cold fingers cramped.

Flashing out of nowhere, a deer bounded across the road. Kylie slammed on her brakes, missing the animal by inches as she spun out of control. She swallowed a scream as the station wagon made a 180-degree turn and came to rest with the car facing back the way she'd come. Shaking, she rested her forehead on the steering wheel while she waited for her pulse to settle from a thundering gallop to a jittery trot.

Was this near disaster a warning that she should give up and go home? But no, she wasn't a superstitious person. Even if she were, it was Christmas Eve, and she'd vowed to do this one thing for her children.

Steeling her resolve, she put the wagon in reverse, turning by inches until the vehicle was headed back toward Branding Iron. She murmured a half-voiced prayer of thanks that she hadn't been going too fast to stop. Now to find that Christmas tree!

By the time she pulled into the parking lot at Shop Mart, the store was about to close its doors to let the employees spend Christmas Eve with their families. The sun was low in the sky. In an hour, it would be dark. Kylie kept a flashlight in the glove compartment, but her search would be easier with some daylight. There was no time to lose.

There were still cars in the parking lot, and people coming out with loaded carts. She hadn't planned to go into the store, but maybe, if she hurried, she could slip inside and pick up some lights for the tree she'd vowed to find, and a few more presents for her children. She remembered a gift card rack at the end of one aisle. Something to spend on after-Christmas bargains might at least cheer them up a little.

Tonight there were plenty of parking spaces. She pulled into the one that was closest to the building and was just about to climb out of the car when a tall figure loomed above the driver's side window. A gloved hand tapped on the glass. Kylie's heart sank as she glimpsed the insignia of the county sheriff's department on the leather jacket. She rolled down the window. What had she done now?

"What's the matter, officer?" She willed herself not to sound nervous. If Texas cops were as prickly as California cops, she didn't want to get on the bad side of this one. He looked as big as a barn door, so tall that, from where she sat inside her wagon, Kylie couldn't see all the way up to his face.

"License and registration, ma'am." He sounded as tough as he looked. Kylie slid her license out of her wallet, pulled her registration out of the glove box and handed it up through the open window.

"Have I done something wrong?" she asked.

"You're parked in a handicapped stall." He took the papers from her hand. "That's against the law."

Oh, rats! The handicapped sign on the curb was buried in snow, as were the marks on the pavement. And how could she be parked when she was still in the car? But Kylie knew better than to argue with the law.

"So what have you got to say for yourself, Kylie Summerfield?"

"I'm sorry," she said lamely. Only then did something click. True, he had her driver's license, but he'd used her maiden name, sounding as if he knew her—and a teasing note had crept into his voice.

"Ben? Ben Marsden?" She leaned out the window, craning her neck.

"Hi. It's been a while." He was grinning as he returned her papers. "Shane told me you were back in town, but I didn't expect to find you here, on Christmas Eve."

"I'm just running a few last-minute errands," she said. "Sorry about the parking. I didn't see the sign in the snow. I can move my car."

"Not worth the bother. The store's already closed. They're checking people out, but they're not letting anybody in. I thought it might be you when I saw the car, but I wasn't sure till I saw your license. How've you been?"

"I'll be fine once we're settled." Kylie kicked herself mentally for having pulled up to the store. Not only was she losing precious daylight, but if her quest for a tree involved carrying out Plan B, it wouldn't help to have the sheriff know she'd come into town.

"Are you on duty all night?" she asked Ben.

"Off tonight after seven. But I'll be working tomorrow."

"Christmas day? That doesn't seem fair."

"Somebody's got to do it. Better me than the men with families."

She was fumbling for some excuse to leave when the sheriff's cell phone rang. He raised it to his ear. "Okay. I'm on my way." He turned to go, then glanced back at Kylie. "Busy night. Maybe we can catch up sometime. Merry Christmas."

"Sure, same to you." As he strode toward his vehicle, Kylie rolled up her window and pulled out of the parking stall. Seeing Ben again would have been a pleasant surprise at any other time. But twilight was closing in. Soon it would be dark, and she still needed to find a tree.

She tried the schools first. The Dumpster for Branding Iron Elementary was behind the lunchroom. Kylie spotted the discarded Christmas tree right away, its stump sticking out of the top. But even from the car, she could see that it was already brown, too far gone for her to waste time on a closer look.

The tree behind the combined middle and high school looked more promising. But when Kylie found a wooden box to stand on and looked into the Dumpster, she realized that someone had used the school parking lot to change the oil in his car. He'd tossed the used oil in the Dumpster. It had oozed all over the tree.

Spirits sagging, she drove back downtown. She'd hoped this errand would be easy. But she'd been wrong, and now it was getting dark fast.

The local bank might have thrown out a tree before closing. Full of hope, she drove around the block and into the alley behind the bank building. No tree. But there was a trail in the snow and a scatter of green needles, where someone had dragged one away. At least some needy family was enjoying a Christmas tree tonight. But she was running out of options, and the light was fading by the minute.

Who else might throw out a tree before Christmas Eve? Her mind made a desperate list. The post office? But they wouldn't have put up a tree. The medical clinic? No, they'd still be open for emergencies; and if they had a tree, they'd likely keep it.

The city hall had always displayed a tree. But when Kylie drove past the place, she saw tree lights glowing through the front window. And there'd been nothing behind the community church. If the Ladies Auxiliary had put a tree in the foyer, they would almost certainly keep it there through the holidays.

Feeling the throb of an oncoming headache, she pulled into a vacant parking lot to think. She'd promised herself that she wouldn't come back without a Christmas tree for Hunter and Amy. But she'd looked every place she could think of. So far, she'd failed to find one.

It was time to consider Plan B.

Kylie knew where to find pine trees. She'd driven past the city cemetery on her way into town. The stand of pines at the far west end of the cemetery was just as she remembered, except that the old trees were bigger. Likewise, the smaller, younger trees were so numerous that they made a miniature band of forest between the cemetery and the hay fields that lay beyond.

Surely, nobody would miss just one.

Kylie had never knowingly broken a law in her entire life. But desperate times called for desperate measures.

The winter twilight was deepening into night as she pulled out of the parking lot. *Desperate times, desperate measures.* The words echoed like a mantra as she switched on her headlights and drove down Main Street toward the cemetery on the far side of town. She wasn't doing this for herself. She was doing it for her precious children.

By the time she pulled off the road by the cemetery, it was black night. But even without a moon, Kylie could see the dark line of trees against the snow, which by now had blown into deep drifts. Thank goodness she'd worn her boots and brought her gloves.

Steeling her resolve, she found Shane's folding saw, turned on her flashlight, and climbed out of her station wagon. It was getting late, she reminded herself. Muriel and the children would be getting worried. There could be no time to waste looking for the perfect tree. She would take the first presentable one that was easy to reach and small enough to cut and drag back to the car. The tree might not be spectacular. But it would be fresh, fragrant, and *real*.

The night was bitter cold. Her breath formed white puffs of vapor as she labored through the deep snow. Where the drifts had piled high against the barbed-wire fence, she managed to climb over, catching her jeans, pulling them loose, and feeling them tear before she tumbled down the drift on the other side.

Clambering up from her knees, she floundered on. Her face was numb; her hands were freezing through her gloves. But she'd finally reached the pines. She could make out individual trees in the darkness, including one that looked like it might do. She checked it with the flashlight. There wouldn't be time to dig down to the base of the tree. She would have to cut it off at the snow line. But from what she could see of it, the top had a nice shape—and, anyway, she was too exhausted to keep looking.

Moving in closer, she shook the weighted boughs, sending snow showers over her clothes and boots. When she'd cleared off as much as she could, she stuck the base of the flashlight into the snow, unfolded the saw blade from its handle, knelt in the snow, and groped under the tree for a place to cut. Pinewood was soft, with the trunk no thicker than her forearm. It shouldn't take long to cut the tree down, load it in the back of the station wagon, and head for home.

Her conscience whispered that she was breaking the law, taking something that wasn't hers. But when she thought of Amy's tear-filled eyes and Hunter, trying so hard to be a man, Kylie knew she had to do this.

Working the saw blade against the trunk, she drew it back and made the first cut. The cold air was making her nose drip. She paused to wipe it with the back of her glove.

The spotlight that struck her eyes turned everything a blinding shade of white. Kylie's hand jerked up to shield her eyes against the glare. For the space of a breath, she was bewildered. Then, as she glimpsed the flashing blue and red lights from the road and realized what was happening, her heart plummeted.

"Put down your weapon," a gruff male voice boomed. "Hands up, where we can see them. You're under arrest."

As promised, Shane had brought his guitar that night for the Christmas songs. With Muriel, Henry, and the children singing along in various keys, he'd fumbled his way through "Jingle Bells," "Silent Night," and "The Little Drummer Boy." But no one was in much of a mood for singing—not when one silent question hung over the dismal little celebration.

Where was Kylie?

Muriel glanced at the mantel clock. "Kylie told me she'd be running errands in town. But it's almost eight. No stores would be open tonight. I'm wondering if she had car trouble."

"Maybe she ran into an old friend." Henry tried to sound cheerful. "She went to school with a lot of people in this town."

"She's not answering her cell phone," Hunter said. "I've tried to call her, but it just rings. Maybe she forgot to charge it."

"I'm getting worried." Amy voiced everyone's fear. "What if something's happened to her?"

Shane rose from his seat on the couch. "I warned her about those bald tires. She could've slid off the road and gotten stuck in some snowbank. I'm going to drive out and look for her. The rest of you stay here in case she calls or shows up. Hunter, you've got my cell number. Call if you hear anything, and I'll do the same."

Lifting his sheepskin coat off the rack, he slipped it on and walked calmly out the back door. He didn't want to alarm the others, but a mother as dutiful as Kylie wouldn't just lose track of time on Christmas Eve. Something was wrong.

Worry gnawed at him as he climbed into his pickup, fastened his seat belt, and started the engine. If he had to venture a guess, it would be that her station wagon had slid off the road or broken down and was stranded somewhere. But if that was the case, why hadn't she used her cell phone? What if she was hurt or trapped? What if she'd decided to leave the car and find help—an open invitation to danger on a dark, freezing night?

As he drove, scanning the sides of the road, Shane mouthed a silent prayer. He tried to think good thoughts, to imagine finding her safe, then holding her close and chiding her for making her loved ones worry. Damn it, she had to be all right. How could he stand it if anything happened to that woman?

Kylie had come to mean a lot to him, he realized. The notion of leaving her and her children was becoming harder to live with every day.

He remembered seeing Amy, slipping out of the shed behind the others with that guilty smile on her face.

Then, when he'd found the axle and confronted her about taking it, she'd stepped up and given him a piece of her mind. Her childish wisdom had left him smarting and strangely moved. Kylie's daughter wanted him to stay—enough to pull a prank that might keep him from leaving. That meant a lot.

And it wasn't just the children. Henry and Muriel had both been on his case. Could they be right? If he left Branding Iron, would he be riding away from his best chance at happiness?

But never mind all that. The one person who mattered most had yet to give him a word of encouragement. Kylie seemed resigned to the idea of his going, almost as if she didn't care.

Yet, he'd caught signs that she *did* care—her passionate response to his kisses, the way she looked at him. . . . Maybe she was holding back because she thought he was going to leave. She'd lost one man she loved. It made sense that she'd be wary of a second loss.

Would it make a difference if she knew he might stay for her? Did he have the courage to take that chance, especially with a widow who seemed to consider herself still married?

One thing was certain. They couldn't continue in this limbo of game playing. When he found Kylie—*if* he found her—he would do his best to open up and be candid about his feelings, something he'd never done with any woman in his life.

He was halfway to town, still searching the roadsides for any sign of Kylie's station wagon, when his cell phone rang. His pulse lurched. Was Kylie all right? Had she made it home? Fumbling for the answer button, he took the call.

"Shane, this is Ben Marsden." Shane recognized the voice of the county sheriff.

"What is it, Ben?" Shane's heart was pounding. Had something happened to Kylie? Could she have been in an accident?

"I was wondering if you'd checked your tools lately," Ben said.

"My tools? What's this about? I'm out here on the road looking for Kylie. She drove into town and she hasn't come back."

"Relax," Ben said. "I saw her earlier at Shop Mart. She's fine."

Shane felt his nerves unclench, but he still didn't know why the sheriff was calling about his tools. And how did Ben know Kylie was fine now? Nothing was making sense.

"Hear me out," Ben said. "I'm home now, but I just got a call from one of my deputies. A woman they booked tonight was armed with a saw when they picked her up. She's refusing to say a word, but after she was booked and put in lockup, one of them recognized your initials on the handle."

"Wait a minute—are you saying they've got Kylie? She's in jail? Damn it, Ben—"

Ben chuckled. He actually seemed to be enjoying this. "Blond, blue-eyed, a real looker, my deputy said. It's Kylie, all right. They found her I.D. in her purse. But like I said, the lady isn't talking. She's refusing to let us call anybody. That's why they called me. And that's why I'm calling you."

Shane shook his head, not knowing whether to laugh or swear. *Kylie in jail? Unbelievable!* "It's all right, Ben. It's fine that she borrowed my saw. I'll come by the jail and pick her up."

"I'm afraid it's not that simple. There are charges pending against her. She'll need to make bail."

"Charges? Hell, Ben, that woman doesn't even jaywalk. What charges?"

"I guess we can drop petty theft for the saw. But there's still trespassing, as well as destruction of city property—that's the big one. Oh, and parking on the wrong side of the road. We had to tow her vehicle to impound."

" 'Destruction of city property'?" Shane cursed under his breath. There had to be some kind of misunderstanding. "What the hell did she do?"

"The deputies caught her at the city cemetery sawing down a pine tree."

"Lord, have mercy!" Suddenly it all made sense—the limits to which Kylie would go to give her children a good Christmas, complete with a real Christmas tree.

"Can't you just call your deputies back and tell them to let her go?" Shane demanded. "The woman isn't a criminal. She's no danger to anybody, including herself. She can come back in and straighten out this mess after the holidays. Besides, it's Christmas Eve! Her children are waiting at home!"

There was a pause before Ben spoke. "I'm sorry, Shane. The people of this county elected me to uphold the law. That doesn't include bending it to do favors for friends, not even you. This has to be done by the book."

"I understand," Shane said, and he did. His friend was a by-the-book kind of man. It was one of the qualities that made him a good sheriff.

"Call me if there's a problem," Ben said. "I'm in my sweats with a cold beer in my hand and a good Western on TV. But I can show up if I have to."

"Don't worry, I'll handle it," Shane said. "Thanks for letting me know."

Ending the call, he checked the impulse to stomp the gas pedal to the floor. The road was slippery, and Kylie wasn't going anywhere. She was perfectly safe.

A smile twitched the corners of his mouth. The smile stretched to a grin. Then laughter bubbled out of his chest and shook his belly.

Perfect little Kylie Summerfield Wayne. For the sake of her children's Christmas, she'd finally done the unthinkable. She'd broken the law, gotten busted, and ended up in jail.

The truth slammed him like a lightning bolt.

Heaven help me, I love her.

There were two women in the holding cell with Kylie. One was barely more than a girl. Dressed in ragged jeans, her hoodie drawn around her face, she sat huddled in the corner with her knees pulled tight against her chest. Was she drugged? Sick? Did she need anything?

Kylie touched her shoulder. "Are you all right?" she asked.

"Leave me alone, bitch!" the young woman snarled.

Kylie drew back like she'd been singed. No one had ever spoken to her that way. But then, she'd never been in jail before.

"Leave her be. That little chick's in here for dealin' meth. She's in big trouble. Nothin' we can do." The other woman was leaning against the wall. She was in her late forties, with bleached blond hair, Dolly Parton makeup, and a plump body crammed into black stretch pants and a skintight sweater. Kylie's mother would have branded her a "floozy." But at least she was friendly.

"First time in here, honey?" she asked.

Kylie nodded.

"What'd they bust you for? Impersonating a Barbie doll?"

"Not quite." Kylie chose to ignore the good-natured jab. "I was arrested for cutting down a tree in the cemetery—or at least trying to."

The woman stared at her, then doubled over, quaking with laughter. Only then did Kylie realize she was drunk. "Cuttin' down a tree—and in the cemetery! Now, there's a new one!" She clutched her knees. "Oh, Lordy, stop me! I'm gonna pee my pants!"

"It wasn't that funny," Kylie said. "My children needed a Christmas tree. I couldn't find one anywhere else."

The woman straightened and wiped her eyes. "Well, good for you, honey. It wouldn't do to let your kids go without a tree on Christmas, would it? Too bad you got busted. Now, less'n somebody springs you, they won't have a tree for Christmas or a mom, either."

Kylie blinked back tears. She'd been too embarrassed to call anybody for help or to give the deputies any personal-contact information. What would Muriel think? What kind of example would she be setting for her children?

She knew they'd be worried about her by now, but there had to be a way out of this. Surely, the sheriff would let her go. He wouldn't keep a mother away from her children on Christmas Eve.

But the woman's remark had slapped her with the cold shock of reality. Unless some miracle happened, she wouldn't be getting out of here tonight.

"Sit down, sweetie. You look ready to drop." The woman guided Kylie to one of the benches that lined the wall of the holding cell. She smelled of whiskey and stale tobacco; right now, she was the closest thing to a friend Kylie had. "Looks like we'll be stuck here awhile. I'm Francine."

"I'm . . . Kylie." She checked the impulse to give a fake name. "How about you, Francine? What are you doing here?"

Francine laughed. "Oh, the usual. Some jerk down at the pool hall thought he could put his hands anyplace he wanted. I taught him different. Whacked him with a bottle. Started a free-for-all. It was fun while it lasted. Kinda hoped I'd end up here for the night. Better than spending Christmas alone in that rat hole where I bunk."

"Hey, Francine!" a male voice called from beyond the door to the office. "We're orderin' pizza. What's yer pleasure?"

Francine glanced at Kylie, one eyebrow raised in question. Kylie shrugged. "Whatever."

"Hawaiian," Francine yelled. "Make it an extra large." She turned back to Kylie. "See, I got good buddies here. Not the worst place to spend Christmas Eve."

"For you, maybe." Kylie couldn't help it. A tear escaped one eye and trickled down her cheek. She wanted to be out of here, with her children, with Muriel and Henry . . . and with Shane.

Suddenly the ache of missing him was more than she could stand. She wanted to curl up in his arms and feel safe, to swim in his clean, leathery man-scent and be swept away by the raw power of his kisses. And she wanted more. She wanted *him*—and the forbidden passions she hadn't known since her marriage. She wanted to wake up to his sleeping face on the pillow, to feel the sweet burn of his unshaven stubble on her skin. She was tired of being good, tired of playing the virtuous, grieving widow. She wanted to feel alive again.

Kylie forced her thoughts back to the present. It was easy to dream from behind bars. But right now, she had more urgent concerns. How was she going to get out of here? Maybe it was time to shake her fist and demand a lawyer.

But who would she know to call? And what lawyer would drive over dark, icy roads to help her on Christmas Eve? All she'd wanted was to make her children happy. Instead they would remember this as the worst Christmas of their lives—a Christmas with no green tree and no presents, a Christmas with their father gone and their bungling, inept mother in jail.

How could she have made such a mess of things?

"Don't look so sad, honey." Francine patted her shoulder. "Christmas is just another day. You'll get through it fine. So will your babies. You'll see."

"Thanks, Francine. I wish I could believe that." Kylie used the back of her hand to wipe away the salty tear that had trickled down her cheek.

"I have a daughter who'd be about your age," Francine said. "Maybe a little younger. But I like to think she'd be pretty like you. She might even have kids of her own by now."

Kylie sensed a sad story behind Francine's words. "What's your daughter's name?" she asked.

"In my memory I call her Annie," Francine said. "But I wasn't allowed to name her for real. By the time she was born, I'd already signed the adoption papers. Only got to hold her once. But she had big, blue eyes, a lot like yours—and a full head of the reddest hair you ever saw."

"And you don't know where she is or who her parents are?"

Francine shook her head. "The parents made sure it was a closed adoption. They were afraid I might try to get her back. And I might've, too. But it wouldn't have been a good idea. I was a little crazy back in those days." She laughed, tossing her bleached blond hair. "Guess I pretty much still am."

"I'm sorry." Kylie couldn't think of anything else to say.

"Don't be, sweetie. I like to tell myself that having that little girl was the best thing I ever did, and that somewhere she's happy."

Kylie's misted eyes blurred her vision. She ought to count her blessings, she told herself. This was a bad time, but at least when she got home, her children would be waiting. She would hug them till her arms ached.

"Mrs. Wayne?" The deputy's nasal voice startled her. She turned around to see him unlocking the cell door. "Your bond's been paid. You're free to go."

Her first reaction was bewilderment. She hadn't told a soul she was here, and she hadn't shared any phone numbers. But as she stepped through the door and glimpsed the tall, lean figure waiting in the hallway, she knew that, somehow, Shane had found her.

Willing herself not to run to him, she turned back toward the bars of the cell. "Will you be all right, Francine?" she asked. "Is there anything I can do? Anybody I can call?"

"Bless you, sugar, I'll be just fine. Go home to your babies, and have a merry Christmas!"

The young woman in the hoodie hadn't stirred.

Knowing there was nothing to be done for her, Kylie walked out into the hall.

Shane was waiting for her, dressed in his sheepskin coat and holding her purse. His face wore a knowing smile. "Let's go home, little jailbird," he said. "You've had quite an evening."

"No comment." Kylie took her purse and fell into step beside him. "Just get me out of here."

They walked outside. The night was black and cold, the stars like pinpoints of ice. He took her arm to steady her going down the front steps.

"I called your family," Shane said. "They were relieved to hear you were safe. You gave them quite a scare."

"Did you tell them what happened?"

"I told them you had car trouble and your phone wasn't working. Unless you want to share the truth, this escapade will be our little secret."

"Thanks." Kylie began to breathe again.

"Your car's in impound," he said, unlocking the passenger door of his pickup. "You won't be able to get it out till Monday. And, of course, there'll be a court date. Knowing the judge, I'm guessing they'll slap you with a fine and probation, maybe some community service."

"That sounds like a bit much, since I barely scratched that poor tree."

"But a scratch is proof of intent. And they're keeping my saw as evidence. Branding Iron justice is like tough love. Believe me, I know." He offered his arm to help her climb inside. Kylie's knees felt wobbly. She slumped against the back of the seat. By the time Shane climbed in on the other side, she was fighting tears and losing the battle.

"Oh, blast it, Shane! I've made such a mess of things! All I wanted was to give my children a good Christmas with a tree and presents. Now they've got no presents, no tree, and almost no mother. Instead of celebrating Christmas Eve, they had to spend it worrying about me—not to mention all the trouble I put you through tonight. How much was my bond? I'll pay you back. I can write you a check."

"Come here, Kylie." Leaning over the truck's console, he reached out and pulled her close. "I don't give a damn about the bond," he muttered. "I don't give a damn about the tree or the jail or the time it took to track you down. All I care about right now is that you're safe and you're here. And if you're wondering why, it's because I care about *you*."

His kiss caught her off guard. Deep and hot and passionate, it was everything a kiss should be. Her pulse skyrocketed. A bonfire flamed inside her as her mouth molded to his heat, lips softening, opening. His breath roughened as he pulled her tighter. His hands found their way under her coat; his touch was waking tremors of long-denied need. She moaned, pressing against him, hungry for more.

A belly jab from the gearshift knob broke the spell. He released her with a sigh. "To be continued—if that's really what you want. For now, let's get you home."

Starting the engine, he swung the truck out of the parking lot. Still reeling from his kiss, Kylie fastened her seat belt and sank back into the leather upholstery. She had no words for what had just happened. Shane was in the driver's seat now—both literally and figuratively.

He drove in silence. Not until after they'd left the town behind did he clear his throat and speak. "This isn't easy to say, Kylie. I'm a proud man, and I don't believe in telling pretty lies to a woman just to get what I want. I care about you and your children, maybe more than I should."

"My children feel the same about you," Kylie said. "You've been wonderful with them. I appreciate that."

"Let me finish. This isn't about your children. This is about you. You know I've been planning to sell out and leave."

"Yes, of course I do."

"To tell the truth, I've been having second thoughts. Muriel and Henry have both tried to convince me to stay, at least long enough to figure out where you and I are headed."

Kylie's heart slammed. She'd fantasized about

a relationship with Shane. But what he was offering was a chance at the real thing. Could she handle it? Was she ready? Shane was everything she could want in a man, the whole package, with kisses that burned all the way to her soul.

So, why was she suddenly terrified?

She forced herself to speak. "So, where *are* we headed, Shane?"

"That's up to you. Give it some thought before you answer. All I ask is that, if it's yes, you'll let me know in time to cancel the listing on my ranch. I don't want those folks in Michigan to make a trip for nothing."

Part of her wanted to say "yes" right now. But that would put so much at risk—the loss, the hurt, the heartbreak. And not only for herself, but also for her children.

"So, what if I say yes and it doesn't work out?" she asked.

"Then we cut our losses and go on with our lives. I'm aware that you're still mourning your husband, Kylie. If you'll give me a chance, I promise to take things slow. I just need to know whether you're willing to try."

They fell silent as they neared the farm and turned in through the front gate. As Shane pulled to a stop, Kylie saw Muriel waiting in the circle of the back porch light, the afghan clutched around her shoulders. Jumping out of the truck, Kylie ran to her.

"Thank heaven you're all right!" Muriel's frail arms went around her for a tight hug. "We were so worried."

"Where are Amy and Hunter?" Kylie asked. "Do they know what happened?"

"I sent them to bed as soon as we heard that Shane had found you. They were both worn-out."

"They must not have had much of a Christmas Eve. Did the package with the presents ever show up?" Kylie was aware of Shane, standing behind her.

Muriel shook her head. "I'm afraid not. But I do have a bit of good news. I found your wedding ring."

"Oh!" In all the excitement, Kylie had almost forgotten about her missing ring. "Where on earth did you find it?"

"I keep a pair of old wool gloves in the pockets of my coat. Your ring was inside one of the fingers."

Kylie remembered now. She'd worn the coat outside and put on the gloves to shovel snow while she spoke with Shane. When they'd ended up arguing, she'd pulled off the gloves and stuffed them back in the pockets, too upset to notice that she'd pulled off the ring as well.

"Here you are, dear." Muriel held out the ring. "I even shined it up a little for you."

Kylie slipped the gold band back on her finger.

"Thank goodness! I was so afraid it was lost forever!"

Behind her, Shane was silent—too silent, Kylie realized. Was something wrong?

"Won't you come in, Shane?" Muriel asked. "I can rustle you up some leftovers if you're hungry."

"I need to be going." His voice was flat, almost cold. "Good night and have a merry Christmas tomorrow."

Muriel stood looking after him as the truck roared out of the gate. "Now what was that all about?" she mused. "He acted as if he couldn't wait to get out of here."

Kylie glanced down at her wedding ring. Chilled by the night air, it felt cold and heavy against her skin. She twisted it around her finger, wondering as her mind circled the truth.

Why had Shane left so suddenly?

Was it because of her?

Was it because, in an instant's thoughtless act, she'd already given him the answer he was waiting to hear?

I know you're still mourning your husband, Kylie . . .

Shane's words came back to her as she stood on the back porch, the cold wind chilling her face. Tonight Shane had swallowed his pride and laid it all on the line, offering to put off his long-held dream for the chance to build a life with her and her children.

233

What had it taken for him to make that offer—how much soul-searching, how much sacrifice? He hadn't told her he loved her, but surely there'd been love behind every word he'd spoken.

She should have accepted his offer right then. Instead she'd hesitated. Then minutes later, like the fool she was, she'd exclaimed over her recovered ring and put it right back on her finger.

No wonder Shane had left so abruptly. As far as he was concerned, he had his answer, and he was finished with her. She would never again feel his arms around her, never again know his kisses. And she would never know the life they might've had together.

"You're shivering," Muriel said. "Let's go inside. You must be half frozen. What happened to your car?"

"It just . . . wouldn't start. I should never have driven it into town." At least the second part was true. She hated lying to Muriel. Maybe later she'd tell her the truth. But right now all she wanted was to forget tonight had ever happened.

"Are you hungry? I can warm you up some dinner."

Kylie shook her head. "Thanks, but I'm too tired to eat. I just want to relax and get warm. Thanks for getting my children through Christmas Eve."

Muriel pulled her close in a hug. "Don't worry,

dear. I know things don't look so good now. But everything will come right in the end. You'll see."

Kylie gazed past the old woman's shoulder at the forlorn silver tree and the bare floor beneath it. Muriel's words were meant to cheer her. But she'd stopped believing in Santa a long time ago.

Chapter Twelve

Shane tapped the brake, easing the truck to a stop on the snowy road. A wide-eyed doe and her gangly half-grown fawn stood frozen in his headlights, too startled to move. He watched them a few seconds before his light rap on the horn sent them bounding into a roadside thicket. Shifting down, he drove on toward home. He could only hope the deer were finding enough to eat on this cold Christmas Eve.

For him, spending the holiday alone would be nothing new. This year he'd hoped to have more exciting plans. But Kylie had made her message clear when she'd slipped that ring back on her finger. She still thought of herself as a married woman, and her war hero husband was still the man in her life.

Getting over her would take time. Her beauty, courage, and womanly spunk had crept into his heart and now refused to leave. The mental picture of her sneaking into the cemetery with a saw to cut down a Christmas tree made his mouth twitch in a wistful smile.

It was a good thing he hadn't told her he loved her. If he had, the blow to his masculine pride would have been too much to stand. At least he'd been able to make a dignified exit.

But it wasn't just Kylie who'd invaded his heart. Her children had found a place there, too. He remembered Hunter hiding from the bikers, then calling him "Dad" as they left the café. And he remembered Amy, her innocent little smile as she stole out of the shed after hiding the bike's front axle.

"It's not fair!" Amy's cry of complaint echoed in his memory. And it *wasn't* fair. Those two great kids had been through a rough time, losing their father, losing their house, and being uprooted from their schools and friends to this cold, lonely place that was nothing like home.

They deserved far better than the Christmas they were getting. But for all their mother's desperate efforts, they would wake up tomorrow to an ugly tinfoil tree with no presents underneath. That, along with the memory of happier Christmases with their father, would make for a sad, dreary day.

Kylie had given it her all, but nothing had worked out as she'd hoped. Now, with Christmas morning hours away, she'd run out of options.

But had he?

As Shane turned in the gate to his ranch, an idea struck him—an idea crazy enough to make him wonder if he was losing his mind.

Why not? he asked himself. Maybe he wasn't the man for Kylie. But he cared deeply about her and about her children. Before he started packing to leave, he would give them a bang-up Christmas, one they would never forget.

Most of what he needed he already had. And what he didn't have he could borrow from Abner Jenkins, his neighbor to the north.

Could he really do this? But there was no time to answer that question. The plan he had in mind would take hours of work to carry out. He needed to get started now.

Stopping the truck in front of his house, he reached for his cell phone and made a call.

Amy and Hunter had hung their traditional Christmas stockings by the fireplace. Kylie filled them with the candy and trinkets she'd bought at Shop Mart. Better than nothing, she thought, but not by much.

She'd used the tracking app on her phone to check the progress of the missing package. The message that came up: Delivery delayed by weather. We apologize for any inconvenience.

"Inconvenience" didn't begin to cover it.

Muriel had said that Christmas shouldn't be about gifts, but try telling that to an unhappy pair of kids who were used to getting what they wished for.

Muriel had long since gone to bed. The children, too, had been asleep when she'd last looked in on them. Kylie was alone in the parlor with the dying fire and the sad silver Christmas tree. Sinking onto the couch, she buried her face in her hands.

She'd knocked herself out, trying to provide a good Christmas for her children, but nothing had worked. The presents were still AWOL, and her efforts to get a real tree had landed her in jail. If Shane hadn't shown up and bailed her out, she'd still be behind bars, sharing Hawaiian pizza with Francine and the deputies.

She remembered Shane's soul-searing kiss and his offer to put off leaving while they tested their relationship. Saying what he'd said couldn't have been easy. He'd put his heart on the line and invited her to two-step on it.

What had she done?

By the time he got her home tonight, she'd been too tired to think straight. When Muriel held out the ring, it had seemed the most natural thing in the world to slip it back on her finger. Only after it was too late did she understand the message her gesture had sent Shane.

Shane Taggart was a proud man. After what she'd done to his male ego, she couldn't imagine he'd give her—or any woman—a second chance.

There was nothing to do but face the truth. Whatever future they might've had, she'd just blown it out of the sky.

December 25

The mantel clock struck twelve midnight. It was Christmas—the first minute of a day Kylie already wished to be over. Rising off the couch, she yawned, unplugged the tree lights, and headed upstairs to bed.

On the way down the upstairs hall, she paused to check on her children. Hunter and Amy were sleeping soundly, both too old to dream of sugarplums. They'd already learned how life can hurt and disappoint you, even when you don't deserve it.

In her room, she switched on the bedside lamp, peeled off her clothes, and slipped her warm nightgown over her head. Brad's silver-framed picture sat on the nightstand. He'd been photographed in uniform. With his beret and his medals, he looked every inch the perfect officer. But his eyes were the eyes a nineteen-year-old girl had fallen in love with. She would always see him in her children's faces and hold him in her heart. But as she sat on the edge of the bed, looking at that handsome, stubborn face, something told Kylie it was time to say good-bye.

She wasn't doing this for Shane, she told

herself. She couldn't assume Shane would ever forgive her. Most likely, he would go away and never come back. But he had opened her to the sweet roller-coaster thrill of loving again. It was a precious gift—a gift that had set her free to move on with her life. Whatever happened, she would always be grateful.

Blinking away a tear, she rose, walked to the dresser, and opened her jewelry box. Sliding the gold band off her finger, she slipped it into a tiny silk bag and laid it in a hidden compartment of the box. She would save it—perhaps for Hunter to give to the girl he would marry one day. But she would never wear it again.

It was time to put Brad's picture away as well. Kylie wrapped it in the silk scarf he'd sent her for her birthday and tucked it into the bottom dresser drawer. That done, she turned down the bed, slid between the sheets, and lay sleepless as the early dawn of Christmas crept around her.

The children would notice that Brad's picture was missing and that she wasn't wearing her ring. But something told her they would understand.

Still on his feet, Shane stood by the kitchen counter, gulping down a second cup of coffee. Glimpsed through the west window, a streak of dark sky was fading to gunmetal gray above the flatland. He'd been up all night, working so hard in the bitter cold that he ached in every bone, joint, and muscle. But the surprise he'd prepared was almost ready.

Abner Jenkins had been glad to lend him what he needed. As for the rest, his mother had left boxes of lights, tinsel, and ornaments in the attic—enough to decorate a forest, as his father had always said. Shane had used everything he found.

It was early still, and he was so tired he could barely stay awake. But if he tried to rest, he might nod off and sleep through the morning. Best to stay awake and get an early start on the chores.

By now, the path through the snow to the barn was well trampled. Inside, Abner's two big gray Percherons, which their owner used to pull the sleigh in the Christmas parade, were munching hay in the spare stalls, where Shane had put them last night. He gave them fresh water and poured them some oats before tending to his own horses. Then he scattered grain for the chickens and gathered the eggs in a wire basket. As he neared the stall where he'd set up the puppy box, Sheila trotted out to greet him. Crouching in the straw, Shane stroked her beautiful head. "How about it, girl?" he murmured. "Are you anxious to go out and play?"

Sheila thumped her tail. Now that her pups were weaned, one of them already gone, she was getting restless. When he was done in the barn, he would let her outside for a romp in the snow. Days from now, he would take her to the vet and have her spayed. Then, as promised, she would go to young Carl.

Even though he knew she'd have a loving home, Shane would miss Sheila when he was gone. He would miss many things about this place—the sunrise over the high plain, the sound of birdcalls in the morning, the hay fields in summer, and the warm, clean smell of the barn when he came in to do winter chores. He would miss the clear view of the stars at night and the friendliness of his neighbors.

He would miss Muriel and Henry, the closest thing he had to family now. He would miss Kylie's children and the life he might have had with their mother. He had loved Kylie. He would love her for a long time to come. But it was time to move on.

Tomorrow he would go online and start looking for motorcycle parts. If he couldn't find the right ones, he'd be shopping for a new bike to take on the road.

The three pups were curled up in a corner of the big wooden box. They woke, yipped, and came running as Shane poured puppy chow into their bowl. The little females dived into their food, scattering kibble in all directions. Mickey took a few bites, then sat looking up at Shane as if expecting some attention.

Shane scooped him up with one big hand and snuggled the little dog against his chest. His small body was all wiggles and quivers as he thrust upward to lick the rough stubble on Shane's chin.

Shane couldn't help remembering the pup's father. Mick had been the perfect dog: smart, devoted, and fearless. He'd loved riding the country roads perched on the backseat of Shane's bike, his nose resting on Shane's shoulder, eyes closed, nostrils drinking the wind. Little Mickey's blue and brown markings were identical to his father's. He had the same alert look and calm manner. He was Mick's last son. But he wasn't Mick. Expecting him to be exactly the same would be unfair, even cruel.

Lifting the pup, Shane kissed the satiny head and looked into the melting caramel eyes. "What are you trying to tell me, boy?" he murmured. "If you could talk, what would you have to say about wanting to be a motorcycle dog like your old man?"

Mickey licked Shane's nose with his warm little pink tongue.

"Something tells me you and I need to have a conversation." Shane set the pup back in the box to munch up the scattered kibble. "To be continued," he said. Then he whistled for Sheila, found her favorite red ball, and let her outside to play in the snow.

"I was hoping Shane would come by this morning." Muriel glanced up from the bacon she was tending on the stove. "He knew he was invited for breakfast."

Kylie kept quiet as she poured orange juice into the glasses and set them on the table by the plates. She knew Shane wouldn't be here for breakfast, and she knew why. But the less said about it, the better.

"You've taken off your ring, I see," Muriel said.

"Yes, I've put it away for safekeeping. I didn't want to take a chance on losing it again." It was, at least, a half-truth.

"A very good idea, dear." Muriel scooped the bacon onto a tin pie plate, put it in the oven to warm with the biscuits, and began cracking eggs into the skillet. From the parlor came the sound of early-morning Christmas cartoons on TV. Hunter and Amy had been up long enough to get dressed, empty their stockings, and open the warm woolen scarves Muriel had crocheted and wrapped for them. The children were trying to be good sports about the missing presents. But Kylie could see the disappointment in their eyes. This was nothing like the Christmas she'd hoped to give them.

"That smells mighty good, Muriel." Henry had come in the back door with a long, clumsily gift-wrapped bundle under his arm. "This is for you."

Muriel's face lit up. "Thank you, Henry. You can put it under the tree for now. I have something for you, too, but breakfast is almost ready. Would you let the children know?"

With the TV turned off and platters of bacon, eggs, golden biscuits, and homemade strawberry jam on the table, they sat down and joined hands for the blessing on the food. Shane's usual chair was painfully empty. Kylie felt his absence as she reached across the space to join hands with her son. At least she and her children were safe, healthy, and together this Christmas, she reminded herself. That was reason enough to be thankful.

She remembered last night's talk with Francine in the jail. She couldn't even imagine how heartbreaking it would have been, holding a baby and knowing it would be for the last time. Francine had been right. This Christmas would pass, and maybe they would learn some lessons of gratitude for the blessings of a warm roof over their heads, good food to eat, and the love of family.

"Why isn't Shane here?" Amy gazed at the empty chair with her big, sad eyes. "Last night he told us he was coming."

"Running a ranch is a lot of work." Kylie didn't want to lie, but no one at the table was ready to hear the truth. "Maybe he's busy taking care of his animals."

"But if he knew he'd be busy, why did he

promise to be here?" Amy demanded. "What if something's happened to him?"

"Let's give him a little more time, Amy. I heard him promise, too, and Cowboy always keeps his word. It could be he's just slow." Muriel's eyes held a flicker of mystery, almost as if she knew something the others didn't.

"I'm getting worried, too," Hunter said. "If he's not here by the time we're done eating, maybe we ought to phone him."

Kylie's gaze was fixed on her plate, as she nibbled food for which she had no appetite. If Shane didn't show up, her children would have one more disappointment to deal with—and it would be all her fault.

They'd almost finished eating when Amy jumped out of her chair. "I hear horses! And jingle bells!" she exclaimed, running to the front window. "Mom! Hunter! Come and look! It's Santa!"

Catching her excitement, everyone at the table got up and rushed out to the front porch. Coming in through the gate was an honest-to-goodness sleigh drawn by two massive gray horses, with brass bells gleaming on their harnesses. In the driver's seat was a lanky figure dressed in a baggy red Santa suit, topped by a familiar black felt Stetson.

Kylie's breath caught. Tears sprang to her eyes. It was Shane.

Pulling the team up to the front of the house, he tipped his hat. "Is anybody here up for a sleigh ride?"

"Me!" Amy bounced up and down.

"And me!" Hunter raced inside to get his coat, with Amy right behind him.

"Anybody else?" Shane surveyed the three adults on the porch, his gaze meeting Kylie's for no more than a flicker. Close-up he looked as if he hadn't slept all night. His eyes were sunk in shadow. His cheeks showed an unshaven growth of black stubble. How much time and work had it taken him to prepare this surprise for her children?

"I'll come, of course." Kylie willed herself to behave as if nothing had happened between them. "Just give me a second to put on something warm."

"Muriel? Henry? How about you two?" he asked. "There's plenty of room."

Muriel glanced up at Henry. "I think we'll stay here and enjoy some peace and quiet. If you're not back by eleven-thirty, Kylie, I'll start making dinner. You're invited, of course, Shane. We'll be eating around one."

"Thanks, we'll see how the day goes."

Inside the house, Kylie put on her coat and pulled on her gloves. Finding the lacy white scarf Muriel had made her, she looped it around her neck; then she made sure Hunter and Amy were wearing their new scarves, too. Muriel would be pleased to see her gifts, and the scarves would be warm in the sleigh.

The sleigh was large and solid, with brass fittings, like something from the olden days. It had two leather-upholstered bench seats, one in back for passengers and a narrower one in front for the driver. Shane climbed to the ground to help Kylie and her children onto the backseat, to which he'd added some warm blankets and quilts. The morning was sunny but cold, with a light breeze sharpening the chill. Kylie tucked the quilts over and around them while Shane climbed back onto the driver's bench.

"Ready?" he called out.

Amy and Hunter cheered.

"Then away we go!" Shane slapped the reins on the rumps of the big draft horses. They were off in a jingle of harness bells, the sleigh runners gliding over the snow.

It was magical.

"We're flying!" Amy cried as Shane swung the sleigh out of the gate, onto the snowpacked road and urged the team to a brisk trot. There was no traffic on the road this morning, no sound except the muffled plod of massive hooves, the jingle of bells, and the happy laughter of children. The sleigh runners cut the snow so smoothly and silently that it really was like flying.

After the first half hour, they'd begun to feel

the cold. Shane used a side road to turn the sleigh around and head back the way they'd come. Kylie was expecting him to take them home to Muriel's. But when they passed the turnoff to the farm, she realized they were on their way to Shane's ranch.

A few minutes later, they'd turned onto the road that ended in Shane's property. In the distance now, they could see his house—and something else.

"Mom, look!" Amy was trying to stand up in the sleigh, but Kylie's arms anchored her to the seat. "Look! Giant Christmas trees!"

"Oh, wow! Cool!" Hunter exclaimed. "Unbelievable!"

Even at a distance, Kylie could see the stately twenty-foot pines that flanked the front porch of Shane's house. From base to top, they glittered with lights, tinsel, and ornaments. "I couldn't bring these trees to your house," he said. "So I had to bring you here."

A lump rose in Kylie's throat. Shane had done this for her children. It must have taken him most of the night, working in the bitter cold, to decorate both trees. No wonder he looked exhausted today.

It was an act of pure, unselfish love from a man she'd driven away with a single thoughtless gesture. Did it mean he'd forgiven her? But no, this wasn't for her. Today he'd barely looked at her, barely spoken to her. This was all for Hunter and Amy.

Which made it all the more amazing.

Wasn't there anything she could say that would cut through his icy pride and make things better? Wasn't there anything she could do to show how much she wanted another chance with him?

Shane halted the team at the foot of the front walk. Amy and Hunter jumped out of the sleigh and ran to the trees. "They're so beautiful!" Amy was dancing from one tree to the other, beside herself with joy. "They're the most wonderful Christmas trees I've ever seen, and they're alive! I can even smell them!"

"They're pretty cool, all right." Hunter stood back with his hands in his pockets, trying to appear grown-up and detached, but his eyes were wide with boyish wonder. "How'd you get all those decorations up so high, Shane?"

"With a ladder and a long pole."

"I would've helped you if you'd asked me," Hunter said.

"Then it wouldn't have been a surprise."

"It would still have been a surprise for Amy."

"I wish I'd thought of that. Feel free to come and help me take them down next week." Shane climbed out of the sleigh. His gloved hand reached up to balance Kylie as she stepped to the ground.

"Thank you," she whispered. "I can't believe you'd do this for my children."

"And why wouldn't you believe it, Kylie? Do you think you're the only one who cares about giving them a good Christmas?" He turned away without waiting for an answer.

Kylie followed him to the broad, covered porch and mounted the steps behind him. She could tell his pride was still smarting. His manner toward her was as cool as a stranger's. Would it make any difference if she apologized and showed him she was no longer wearing her ring? Or was it too late?

What a careless, insensitive fool she'd been! Shane was everything she wanted in a man, and everything her children needed in a father. If she hadn't realized it before, she knew it now.

What if she'd already lost him?

Amy and Hunter had been taking in the trees, chattering and exclaiming as they dashed back and forth to admire a newly noticed light or ornament. When Shane spoke from the porch, they stopped and stood looking up at him as if he'd hung the moon and stars.

"This skinny Santa's got a present for you," he said. "I couldn't leave it out here under the trees. But I'll give it to you in the house. Come on inside."

Stripping off his gloves, he opened the front door and walked into the house. Wide-eyed, Amy and Hunter raced after him. As they pulled off their coats and gloves, Kylie, coming in after them, could almost read their minds. Shane had given them a sleigh ride and not one but two spectacular Christmas trees. Could anything top that?

In all the years Kylie had known Shane, she'd never been inside his house. The spacious parlor was made homey by well-worn leather furniture and the glowing embers of a blaze in the big stone fireplace. A thick wool rug covered the hardwood floor. The décor, what little there was of it, was tasteful but masculine, without a trace of fussiness. A framed photo of Shane's parents on their wedding day sat on the mantel. Next to it sat another photo, showing a younger Shane on his beloved motorcycle, a beautiful blue heeler dog on the seat behind him.

Amy glanced around the room. "Where's our present?" she asked.

"Amy, where are your manners?" Kylie scolded her gently.

"Sorry." Amy took a seat on the couch.

"Just hang on. It's coming." Shane vanished into the kitchen. An instant later, they heard the quiet opening and closing of the back door. Hunter sat on the couch next to Amy, both of them squirming with excitement. Kylie, still in her coat and gloves, perched on the arm of a chair near the front door. Today was about the children, not about her and Shane.

Seconds, then minutes crawled past before Shane walked back into the room—empty-handed. Hunter and Amy stared at him. Where was their present?

"Sorry." Shane shook his head. "I wanted to tie a big red bow around your present. I tried. But . . . the little critter wouldn't let me."

Something wiggled and whimpered beneath Shane's loose-fitting red Santa suit. Kneeling, he opened the front of the jacket. A little brown-and blue-spotted bundle of fur tumbled onto the rug.

"It's Mickey!" Hunter jumped off the couch and dropped to the floor by the puppy. Shrieking with delight, Amy fell to her knees beside them. The next few minutes passed in a frenzy of giggles and puppy licks and hugs and petting.

Shane had stepped back to watch. Kylie slipped off her gloves and laid them on the chair. This moment was her one chance—maybe the only chance she'd ever have.

Without a word, she rose from the chair arm and moved to stand beside him. Her pulse raced. What would she do if he ignored her? Holding her breath, she slipped her ringless left hand into his. She could only hope he'd feel the difference and understand.

At her first touch, his hand tensed. Was he resisting her or only startled? Daring to go further, she interlaced her fingers between his.

"Thank you," she whispered, "from the bottom of my heart."

His breath caught. Then, as if suddenly aware of her empty finger, his welcoming palm enfolded hers. He glanced down at her and smiled. Kylie began to breathe again.

"I hope the pup's all right with you," he said. "I cleared it with Muriel over the phone early this morning, but I didn't want to tell you and spoil the surprise."

"It's fine," she said. "Not just fine—it's wonderful. I've never seen Hunter and Amy so happy. But I thought you were keeping Mickey to be your motorcycle dog."

"About that." His hand tightened around hers. "Mickey and I had a little talk. I got the impression he wouldn't be happy roaming around the country with an overage biker bum. He wanted to be a kids' dog—a family dog. Anyway, who knows?" He pulled her closer against his side. "If things work out and I decide to finally grow up, I may not be needing that old bike as much as I'd planned."

They rode back to Muriel's in the sleigh, with Mickey snuggled under the blankets and a box of puppy chow and training pads tucked under Amy's feet. Kylie's gaze traced the contours of Shane's back and shoulders as he drove the team. Even in that baggy Santa suit, he was gorgeous.

Just looking at him made her feel as giddy as the teenage girl who'd first fallen in love with the town bad boy. But now, knowing the man he'd become, her love was deeper, stronger, the lasting kind.

Muriel and Henry were waiting on the porch when the sleigh pulled up to the house. Amy nudged her mother. "Look, Mom! They're holding hands!"

Indeed they were. Their faces wore broad smiles as Shane helped Kylie, her children, and their new puppy down from the sleigh.

"We have some news for you," Muriel said as she ushered them into the warm house.

"Did our presents get here?" Hunter asked.

Muriel's blue eyes twinkled. Her cheeks were flushed pink. "Not yet. This is different news. Henry and I are getting married!"

"Wonderful!" Kylie hugged her great-aunt. "I'm so happy for you both!"

"Congratulations." Shane shook Henry's hand. "What brought this about?"

Henry grinned. "All these years, I've never had the courage to propose to her. It was this little mite who got me thinking about it." He nudged Amy's shoulder. "She flat out told me we should get married, and I asked myself, 'Why not? What's an old duffer like me got to lose?' "

Muriel laughed. "I thought he'd never ask me! I said yes so fast it almost bowled him over."

Kylie and Shane took a moment to admire the beautiful wrought-iron coatrack Henry had made Muriel for the entry of the house. Then Kylie helped finish the last-minute dinner preparations and they all sat down to eat. In the joining of hands for grace, they celebrated the shared blessings of the holiday. Everyone at the table had reason to be thankful. At Muriel's urging they went around the table and took turns expressing their thoughts.

"I'm thankful for the spirit of love and friendship in this house," Muriel said, passing the platter of sliced ham to Henry on her right.

Henry speared two slices of ham and put one on Muriel's plate. "I'm thankful for this beautiful woman sitting next to me. And I'm thankful that I won't have to spend the rest of my life sleeping in that ratty old trailer." Realizing what he'd just implied, the old man blushed beet red.

Hunter had already managed to load his plate. "I'm thankful for this food," he said. "And I'm thankful for Shane and all the hard work he did to make this a great Christmas."

Kylie was proud of her son. He hadn't even mentioned the missing presents, which, according to her tracking app, wouldn't be arriving till tomorrow.

Shane cleared his throat, hesitating. "I'm thankful for the first Christmas I've really celebrated in twenty years. Thanks to all of you for finally giving me a reason."

Now it was Kylie's turn. She gulped back the lump in her throat. "I'm thankful for all of you," she said. "Muriel—to you for opening your home to us. Henry, for all your help. Hunter and Amy, to you for soldiering through so many changes. And to Shane—" She glanced at him, knowing that what she really wanted to say was for his ears alone. Her tears welled, her throat choked off. "Oh, drat!" she muttered, dabbing at her eyes with her napkin.

Amy reached over and squeezed her mother's hand. "I thought this was going to be the worst Christmas ever. But it's turned out to be one of the very, very best." She glanced toward the living room. "If Mickey could talk, what do you think he'd be thankful for?"

But Mickey, worn out from so much love and play, had found a warm spot near the fireplace. He was curled up, fast asleep, under the old foil Christmas tree.

An hour later, after the meal was finished and the cleanup done, Shane rose from where he'd been sitting to watch Hunter and Amy play with their new pup. "I need to get the horses and sleigh back to Abner's place," he said. "I'll be picking up my truck over there. Want to come along, Kylie?"

"Sure." Kylie hurried to get her coat and gloves. She needed some time alone with Shane, and since he hadn't invited anybody else, it was likely he felt the same way.

Outside, he helped her onto the driver's bench, climbed up next to her, and laid a quilt over her lap. Taking the team at an easy pace, he drove the sleigh out of the yard and down the lane toward the main road. The light breeze numbed their faces. The late-day sun sparkled on the snow.

"I hope my children remembered to thank you," Kylie said, making conversation.

"Of course they did. They're good kids and you've taught them well." The slanting sunlight etched weary shadows beneath his eyes. He was a tired Santa in a suit too loose for his lean body. Kylie found herself wanting to cradle him in her arms and rub her face against his whiskery chin.

"What you did for them today was . . . unforgettable," she said. "They'll remember this Christmas for the rest of their lives. They'll tell their children about it."

"We'll be getting old by then, Kylie." He stopped the sleigh under the overhanging branches of a willow. "But I hope we'll be together."

He turned on the bench. His arms went around her. His kiss was long and hard and deep. "I've been wanting to do that all day," he muttered as they eased apart.

"Then what do you say we do it again?" She kissed him full out, devouring him with her lips, just as she'd dreamed of doing in her teenage fantasies.

A raven, perched on an overhead branch, croaked and flapped into the air, showering them with snow. Laughing, they fell back against the bench.

Shane righted himself and grinned at her. "There are better places for this when we've got time," he said. "For now, let's go put these horses away."

Kylie snuggled against his shoulder as he drove the sleigh. There was time, she thought. Time to talk, time to plan, time to dream. But she meant to make the most of every minute with her long, tall Santa.

Epilogue

December 25, the next year

The Christmas tree was almost as tall as the ceiling. From its lush, green branches, Kylie's precious family ornaments dangled among showy decorations from Shane's mother's collection. The scent of fresh pine mingled with the aromas of roast beef and fresh hot rolls drifting from the kitchen.

Relaxing on the leather sofa, Shane surveyed the joyful chaos of opened gifts, scattered paper, and trailing ribbons. In the middle of the floor, Amy was giving Mickey a belly rub. The dog's eyes were closed. His tail thumped happily on the carpet.

Mickey had grown up to look exactly like his loyal, obedient father. But he wasn't his father. He was loving and playful, with a goofy streak that kept his young owners laughing—a perfect family dog. Last summer, when Carl had come to work on the ranch, he'd brought Sheila along. Mother and son had enjoyed a tail-wagging reunion, and Sheila had begun teaching her leggy, half-grown pup some herding lessons. Mickey had shown all the right instincts. Come next summer, he'd be full grown and ready to work the cattle like a pro.

Amy gave Mickey's belly a final scratch and scrambled to her feet. "Dad, can I take Mickey out to the barn?" she asked. "He needs a run. And I saved some carrots for the horses, so they could have a Christmas present, too."

"Ask your mother first," Shane said. "She might need your help with dinner."

"I'll ask her. But I already set the table and helped her peel potatoes." She scampered into the kitchen with the dog at her heels. Shane's stepdaughter had taken to ranch life as if born to it. She loved the animals and spent every minute she could spare on horseback. Her favorite Christmas gift had been the beautiful new boots her parents had bought her. Next summer, if she kept her grades up, Shane had promised her a horse of her own.

In a quiet corner of the room, Hunter was playing a game on his new iPad. Sensing his father's eyes on him, the boy looked up, grinned, and went back to his game. Hunter enjoyed riding, too, but seemed happiest working with Henry in the machine shop, learning to weld and tinkering with the wrecked motorcycle, which was coming together in slow stages as parts were repaired or tracked down and replaced. Maybe by the time Hunter was old enough to ride it on the back roads, the bike would be ready for him. That was fine with Shane. He'd moved on to other things, like being a father.

As a parent, he had a lot to be thankful for. Kylie's children had adjusted well, both to the marriage and to their new schools. They were getting good grades, had made some nice friends and both of them were excited about the coming addition to their family.

Two weeks ago, Amy and Hunter had helped him decorate the two big pine trees that flanked the front porch of the house. It had been hard work, hauling strings of lights, tinsel, ornaments,

261

and extension cords up tall, shaky ladders. But the children had wanted to do it. Shane had the feeling it would become one of many family traditions. Life was good. Damned good.

The heat from the fireplace was making him sleepy. It was time he did something useful. Rousing himself off the couch, he strolled into the kitchen, where Kylie was putting the finishing touches on Christmas dinner.

For a moment he paused in the doorway, just taking in the sight of her—the way her blond hair curled softly around her heat-flushed face, the capable movements of her hands, the roundness of her body beneath the loose-fitting blue sweater that matched her eyes. Lord, but she was beautiful. He'd never known how much a man could love a woman till she came into his life.

Stepping behind her, he slid his arms around her swelling waist. The tiny flutter kick against his palm sent a thrill through him that was unlike anything he'd ever experienced. The baby, a boy, was due in three months.

When Shane thought of what he would have missed if he'd followed his dream of roaming the country on his bike, he could only shake his head. He was a happy man, and he owed it all to the blue-eyed angel who'd backed over his motor-cycle, shattered his dream and replaced it with something far better.

"You smell good." He nuzzled his wife's neck. "Could you use some help in here?"

"Your timing's perfect," she said. "Henry and Muriel are on their way over. They'll be here in a few minutes."

"Great!" The whole family looked forward to having Henry and Muriel come for Christmas dinner. The two of them had been married for nearly a year, and they still behaved like honeymooners. There was a new spring to Henry's step, a new sparkle in Muriel's eyes.

"So what do you need me to do?" Shane asked.

"I need you to lift the roast out of the oven. Let it sit a few minutes before you carve it. While you're waiting, maybe you can put some ice in the water glasses. That'll give me time to mash the potatoes and toss the salad. Oh, and Shane—"

"Hmm?" He'd turned toward the oven, but he paused to look back at her. "Anything else?"

"Yes." She strode toward him, seized the front of his flannel shirt, and yanked him close. "Just kiss me, Cowboy."

Center Point Large Print
600 Brooks Road / PO Box 1
Thorndike, ME 04986-0001 USA

(207) 568-3717

US & Canada:
1 800 929-9108
www.centerpointlargeprint.com

12-15
K